I0690610

Clydesdale
& COMPANY

First Edition

Published by The Nazca Plains Corporation
Las Vegas, Nevada
2009

ISBN: 978-1-935509-09-7

Published by

The Nazca Plains Corporation ®
4640 Paradise Rd, Suite 141
Las Vegas NV 89109-8000

PUBLISHER'S NOTE
Clydesdale & Company is a work of fiction created wholly by *Bob Archman's* imagination. All characters are fictional and any resemblance to any persons living or deceased is purely by accident. No portion of this book reflects any real person or events.

Cover Photos, Christopher Howey and Graham Klotz
Art Director, Blake Stephens

Clydesdale
& COMPANY

First Edition

Bob Archman

Part I

The new Police Chief was able to destroy the department in a remarkably short period of time. The last election in Richmond had unusually low turnout and the new Mayor and Council were dominated by born-agains, whose primary interest was in the moral purity of the city. They were worried about homosexuality, abortion and Christian education. They fired the Police Chief who had overseen the reduction of the crime rate by 30% and replaced him with a man named Randall Q. Odinmeyer.

Odinmeyer had no interest in the ability of the Policemen, or women to catch criminals, or deal with crime. He felt sexual and alcohol abstinence and strict monogamy was the prerequisite of serving in the police. Six months later twenty percent of the force was gone. There were several open witch hunts, one of which resulted in the suicide of the Chief of Detectives and soon the department was ruined.

The effect on the crime rate would take several years to determine, but Odinmeyer had the support of the Mayor and the ultra-reactionary newspapers. The general public was unaware of what was going on, for a while at least.

I got out of the force after the Chief's right hand man asked me why I wasn't married, or seeing a girl. I saw the writing on the wall. I have a lawyer friend who told me I could sue their asses, but I didn't want to do that. I'm no virgin and I've been with a lot of guys. Some are out and some aren't. I couldn't expose or embarrass any of them, plus I like being a policeman. If I sued I might never get another job, or would always be "that gay cop."

I'm Wildridge Noland. Everyone calls me "Clydesdale". I'm five-two and 120 pounds, but hung. When I was 14 kids at the showers were calling me a pipsqueak. The coach went by, saw me and my cock and said I looked more like a Clydesdale than a pipsqueak. The name stuck. I found myself 45 years old, with medals and commendations galore from the police force and unemployed. I was drowning my sorrows in the ass of my best friend, John, when he came up with an idea. John's a building contractor, a good one and he's made lots of money. For some reason, he really took a shine to me.

I actually know why he likes me. While I'm a spectacularly unimpressive looking hair ball, my cock is three sizes bigger than my body. The first time I shoved it up his ass, John seemed to glow. I liked it okay. I always like to be appreciated, but the second time I did it, he glowed again and I began to have a warm and fuzzy feeling. The third time, John and I were on the same wavelength. It was a perfect fit. His ass and my cock were made to fuck.

You might think that nine inches of cock in a quivering ass hole is a slender connection on which to base a friendship. You would be wrong. First of all, there is nothing slender about my cock. Secondly, it seems we got to like each other, starting with the cock and moving outwards. We aren't married and we aren't lovers. We are friends who like each other a lot and really like to fuck.

I'm not the kind of guy who spills out his guts and tells everyone his problems. I figure it's my problem and I'll figure a way out of it. John likes to be slow fucked and I like that too. I discovered I tend to be a bit more personal when I'm deep in a guy's ass. Talking takes my mind off the fucking and I can go longer before I shoot. You can't be standoffish when you're talking and rubbing a man's prostate with your meat.

"I don't know what in hell to do," I said. "I guess I could move to a new town, but I've got lots of friends here. I don't know if I want to start again from zero."

"What about the suburban police forces. They need people, don't they?" John asked. He squeezed his ass and it felt great.

"I'm not made to be a traffic cop. I want to catch bad guys, not speeders. That's the problem with the State Troopers too." I gave him a good thrust. I was stroking his cock. I had been thinking of putting some lube on it, but as I thrust, he oozed enough precum to slick it up.

"I can see your point." John agreed with me. "What about becoming a private dick?" I burst out laughing. He looked puzzled and realized what he had said. We both laughed. I pulled out far enough so only the head was in his ass. Then, I thrust deep. As soon as my pubic hair touched his ass, he clamped tight. I slowly pulled out again. By the time I was out, he had pulled my foreskin over the head again. I've got a lot of skin.

"Why don't you run a security service?" he asked. "There must be lots of people and organizations looking for extra protection, especially with this ass hole in charge of the police." I popped through the hole and John's sphincter peeled my skin back. I loved that. It felt great, so I repeated it again.

"I can't see myself looking at I.D.s at the gate of an apartment complex," I said. I loved it when my cock was in to the hilt. John liked it when I was poking half way up his hole with the head giving his prostate a bath in my precum. I always took care of him, unless I shot off too early.

"There must be a lot of people who need more than that. It would be good to have an undercover man in addition to the uniformed man out front. I know the downtown theaters want real protection for their patrons. So do the big civic organizations," John added. I stopped my deep thrusting and massaged his prostate. John stopped talking. He couldn't think when I did that. When I said I liked deep thrusting it didn't mean I didn't like what John liked. It felt good, but wasn't the sort of good that makes you shoot.

John was really enjoying it and I toyed with the idea of pushing him over the edge. I decided to talk more, so I shoved my cock deep and John relaxed some, "Do you think there's a market for that?" I asked.

"You have a great record for catching petty crime, purse snatchers, muggers. They are the people who terrorize the patrons to the theaters, or the ballet. The uniform men at the door help, but the, problem is at the parking decks and lots," John said. "I know all those people. I could get you in touch with them."

"That might work," I said. "I would love to do the special jobs. I'm not sure I'm the kind of guy who inspires confidence. I can do it, but I don't look like the kind of guy who can do it."

"What is Butch doing?" John asked. Butch had been my partner on the force and looked like a recruiting poster for the Marines. "Is he available?"

"He's in the same fucking boat I am in. There are several other guys who might be interested in this too, Roosevelt Jones, Freddy Williams, and Virgil Goodhue. They're all good men," I said. John got me thinking. We were all good men, top notch police officers with a taste for man meat. John's idea made some sense. It wouldn't be easy, but it might work. While I was thinking things over my cock made up its mind and I shot off.

One of the nice things about orgasms is they're always good. You don't build up a tolerance for them like antibiotics, an orgasm is an orgasm. That being said, I had a top of the line, deluxe, A-number One orgasm. It caught me off guard. I drained my balls into his ass and I came damn near shooting a couple of my internal organs through my cock into his love tunnel too.

I'm not a very lovie-dovie guy either, but John and I had some no fooling kissing and hugging time. When I came to my senses I was about to apologize for not getting him off when I realized we were damn near cemented together with his cum. He had shot off while we were kissing. We took a shower and washed it off. Dried cum is a bitch to get out of body hair. We sat down to have a drink. John brought the subject of my future again.

"If you don't mind, Clydesdale, I'm going to call some people up and see what the market is for a new security company," John said. "You talk to

Butch and see what he thinks." John was still leaking a bit from our play time earlier. I licked his cock for a while before we went to bed. I had been feeling down when I dropped in earlier that night. I was feeling real good by the time I fell asleep.

John is a smart man and a good judge of character. That's true even though we are friends. I know I wasn't equipped to be the front man. Butch was. Butch was good looking, muscular and well spoken. He inspired confidence. We are best friends. Butch immediately liked John's scheme and expanded it. Most of the security operations in town were staffed by minimally paid men and women, whose primary function was to call the police when something happened.

Clydesdale & Company provided special services for when one of their clients had trouble. There could be a rapist in a shopping center lot, or a purse snatcher attacking theater patrons. We would work for the security and do some real policing when they had big problems. We knew the men left at the city Police force and knew that some real policing would be needed.

John picked the name, Clydesdale & Company. He wanted to make sure we didn't sound like a security company. We might be a horse supply place, or a sporting goods store. Most of the time we were low profile, pretending to be working for the security company. I have no great respect for the cop-for-hire companies, but I was wrong about that. Most sincerely wanted to protect their clients and most of the old guys who worked as night watchmen were sincere. They just couldn't stay awake all the time and weren't strong enough to do battle with a drugged up perp.

The new Mayor and Police Chief provided our first clients. Because of the loss of personnel in the police department, the Mayor announced that patrols in the restaurant and residential areas would be reduced after 9:00 at night. He volunteered that respectable people should be at home and in bed by then. Richmond isn't New York, but there are a lot of people who are going out to dinner or a club at nine, not coming home. The Mayor scared the restaurant and nightclub owners.

Our first client was a group called "The Western Alliance". It was a joke name too, like Clydesdale & Company. The Western Alliance was a group of civic organizations serving neighborhoods to the west of Downtown Richmond.

They included several commercial associations as well as the prosperous, restored residential areas.

The city had closed the Precinct Station which served the area. This might have been okay, if the City hadn't opened an office to concentrate on fighting cyber porn. They wanted to make sure that 13 year old boys weren't exposed to naked girls on line. It seems to me when I was 13, wanting to see naked girls was about as natural as anything can be for kids that age. I wanted to find pictures of naked men and couldn't find them.

The Western Alliance neighborhoods weren't high crime areas and wanted to make sure they didn't become high crime. These districts felt exposed and threatened.

We rented a storefront off Main Street and set up shop. We asked the President of the Western Alliance over to talk about what we might do for them. Elinor Salina was a beautiful woman, blond, delicate and well dressed. She came with Ari Metropolis, a restaurant owner and President of the West End Merchants Association. He looked like a gorilla.

Butch introduced us and I made a little speech. "Up until this time," I said "I had thought the Mayor was a fool, but I have had to revise my opinion. No mere fool would announce he was reducing police patrols at night. He might as well send engraved invitations to known criminals giving them appointments to rape and pillage." Elinor broke in.

"I don't think he's a fool. He's doing this on purpose," she said. "He wants to punish us for voting against him. He thinks our neighborhoods are populated by feminists and fags and we deserve to be punished."

"I think he's playing to the Bible thumpers in the rural areas. That ass hole wants to be Governor and he wants to destroy us to launch his career," Ari said. "He's reducing police protection so the crime rate will rise. He will say the crime is the result of our immoral ways and close us down. A friend said he was originally planning a curfew. 9:30. He wanted the streets cleared at 9:30!"

"We need to nip this in the bud," Butch said. "Without protection, your neighborhoods are ripe for picking. Our criminal elements will be ready to move in as soon as the Mayor gives the all clear." Butch then outlined a proposal. We were to train citizen patrols and provide muscle for their anti-crime efforts. He figured a combination of increased citizen participation and professional help would solve the problem.

Butch introduced Roosevelt who gave an outline of his training scheme. Roosevelt was a six foot four black man who looked like a professional football player. He was organized and well educated. He proposed a scheme that was sensible and doable. We had all talked about this among ourselves before, but I was still surprised how good it sounded coming from Roosevelt.

He gave a budget. I thought they would walk out the door when they heard it. They didn't even blink. There was some big money in the area and they were scared. They said, "okay". We had our first job.

I walked Eleanor home. She knew I was the guy who had caught the purse snatching ring several years before. I didn't know many women as pretty as she was. She seemed to know her stuff. I didn't know that eventually she planned to run for Mayor and solve the problem from the top.

When I got back to the office Ari was still talking with Roosevelt. Butch had gone home. I lived above the store and I asked them up for a beer. My apartment was basic. I thought of it more as a dorm than a home. As it turned out, my apartment and the office were much more like fire stations, where the firemen sleep above the trucks. I had furniture loaned to me by John and his friends and a simple galley kitchen. The place was straight 'Home Depot' stuff.

The only nice thing in my apartment was the bath and shower. It was a big, walk in type, covered in expensive tile. An old friend put it in for free. I had done him a favor and the tile and the plumbing fixtures were mis-ordered for a big house in the deepest West End. The owner had demanded it and didn't like it when it came. It couldn't be returned, so he had to buy it. My tile friend got it for free. The apartment suited me fine.

Roosevelt was Butch's friend. I knew him, but not very well. Apparently Ari knew him too. After a few beers we all loosened up. Ari went off to the bath to take a leak.

"Where in hell did that come from?" he exclaimed from the bath.

"What?"

"The bath! It looks like it had just escaped from Architectural Digest!" he answered. Roosevelt and I went back to see him. Ari looked dumb-struck as he stood in the middle of the room. A decorator friend said it was Azure blue with celadon highlights and with five foot high tropical birds in bas relief. I thought of it as a blue and green room with pretty birds. Whatever it was, it was nice. The toilet and double lavatory sat behind a short wall. The rest of the room was the shower.

Roosevelt was impressed too. "It's something you'd expect to find in Hollywood," he said. "Does it make you feel like a star? It's unbelievable."

"Can I try it?" Ari asked. I figured he may have had more to drink than I had thought. I said 'sure', there was enough room for half the city. Ari and Roosevelt stripped and I followed suit. I later found out Ari and Roosevelt were a lot closer than I had known and this wasn't the first time they had been naked together. The shower had four heads and a steam feature.

"Where in hell did that come from?" Ari exclaimed again. This time he was looking at my cock. "That's the biggest piece of meat I've ever seen on a white man!" Roosevelt bellowed in laughter.

"I asked Butch how a guy as short as you ever got on the force. He said there was more to you than meets the eye," the black man said. "Shit, half your body weight must be in your cock and balls!" Ari was already on his knees slurping his tongue inside my foreskin.

"I always have trouble with short guys like you," Roosevelt said.

"Why?" I asked. I know all the stories of short guys who want to be Napoleon. I can be a bit aggressive, but I never wanted to conquer the world.

"It hurts my back to get down far enough to suck their cocks," he said. Ari wasn't having any problem at all.

"I bet we can work something out," I said. And we did.

Part 2

It's safe to say that Ari, Roosevelt and I hit it off. Once we got naked it was as if we had been old fuck buddies since our forefathers got off the ark. Roo sat on a ceramic bench in the corner of the shower. Ari just bent over to suck Roo's dark dong and opened his ass nice and wide. I know an invitation when I see it and I shoved my meat in to the hilt. I know a guy doesn't open his hole without an ulterior motive and I was right. Ari liked it in the ass and had no problem with Roo or me.

I'm a real hairy guy and its not often I find someone who is as hairy as me, but Ari was a circus freak in the hair department. I ran my hands through the fur on his back. My hairy balls were bouncing against his gorilla nuts and I got real turned on. I felt like George of the Jungle and I had found true love with Gorilla man.

"I'd like some of that ass," Roo said after a while. I am always polite, so I pulled out, a bit unwillingly and traded places with Roosevelt. Ari didn't mind at all. The steam was going, so it was warm, humid and felt tropical. I fantasized I was in a gay porn movie with an unusually good set. We weren't pretty like the porn stars, but we had enough balls and cocks to satisfy the most rabid size queen.

I felt we had neglected Ari's cock, so I got on the floor. I made Ari and Roo spread their legs so I could get at Ari's meat. The second Roo rammed Ari's prostate I knew this was a good idea. Ari was spread wide and his innards must have shifted to the ideal position.

Sucking Ari was a trip. His balls were big, his cock was short and he could have done his pubic hair up in a bouffant. It wasn't a cock for guys who don't like hair caught between their teeth. When I finally licked my way through the hair forest, the cock was a curiosity. It was a huge, two inch head on a thick, three inch shaft.

Now I have always been interested in cock heads. It seems to me the head is the business end of the cock. It has always seemed odd the part of the cock that gets the most use in sex is also the most sensitive and tender. Someone once told me the prostate is another sensitive part of a guy's sexual anatomy. Ari's cock was dribbling from the first lick. He liked it. I was sucking Ari as Roo pounded his ass and I wondered which activity felt best to him.

Roo was moaning some and I knew he had popped. We rearranged ourselves.

"You've been a trooper, Ari," I said. "What's you pleasure?" He looked at me sheepishly.

"I'd kind of like a little more fucking," he said. "It may be a bit sloppy."

"Shit! We're in the shower!" I said. "Do you mind if I screw you spread-eagled? It gives me a little more control."

"Hot Damn!" he said. Ari was a nice guy. I gave him a good country boy fucking this time. His eyes, tongue and pink cock head were just about the only parts of him not covered in hair. Underneath he had a barrel chest and a six pack gut. He began to shoot and it made a design like one of those Potluck modern paintings. There was pure white cum splattered all over his chest and gut. I was admiring the design when I felt the cum build up in my shaft.

I pulled out and added my seed to the mess. We were both winded. Roosevelt had recovered and was getting hard again. He played with the cum on Ari's body and wrote out the words "wash me" in sperm.

No one ever accused me of being handsome and Ari was not a dream boat in a conventional sense. Roosevelt, however, was beautiful. He was golden brown with a clipped, bushy, jet black mustache and short, almost shaved hair on his head.

He worked out and you could tell. He was sculpted. I guessed he must have shaved his body at one time. There was a short stubble of hair over his chest, but only his pubic hair was bushy. He had a Concord like cock. It looked like that French plane. It stuck straight out then drooped. The Concord goes to a point. Roosevelt's cock flared out into a mushroom head.

His piss slit glistened. I felt it and it was cock slime, just right for easing his way into an ass. Roosevelt was a reserved and in control guy, a real marine type. He didn't show much emotion. Fortunately, his balls must have been permanently in overdrive. When ever I saw him naked, he was dripping. He couldn't control his balls; they loved sex even if he couldn't admit it.

Ari was the opposite. He loved it and you knew it. We got to be good friends. He had a wife and kids and loved them too. She was a semi-invalid and sex with men was his release from being a full time dad, nurse and restaurant owner. I never figured out how he did it.

Our patrol for the Western alliance was good for us. First of all, we did real well. There was a series of muggings the week we were hired and we figured out who was doing it quickly and put the kibosh to it. I had a technique of catching the perps and providing a little punishment too. It's good when you nab a guy in the act and get to apprehend him. A dislocated shoulder, or broken arm can make a guy remember the error of his ways pretty good.

I'm so small most of the idiots were too embarrassed to admit I did it. Even the poor lawyers who got stuck as public defenders knew they would be laughed out of court if they said the 200 pound bruiser was assaulted by this 120 pound twerp. I'm kind of country anyway and in court I come across as a real hayseed.

The Judges like me. They get to see me all the time and I made it easier to sentence the guys. I've already done some punishing. Judge Wilson told me once that he wasn't a fool and I'd better be real careful. I told him I knowed he wasn't a fool and I only tackled guys caught in the act. He didn't go any further, but we understood each other. When a guy showed up in a sling, or cast, they knew I was the apprehending officer. "Clydesdale Casts" were a joke in the judge's chambers someone told me.

The other nice thing about the Western Alliance is the group was made up of a lot of wealthy and well connected people. We kept a low profile. Officially it was the citizens' patrols who made the difference. The important people knew it was us and they came to us for help. We didn't want it to be known there was a private security firm that knew its stuff. The glory went to our clients. We did the work and got the satisfaction. We also made quite a bit of cash in the process.

Two other guys were part of our original operation. Freddy Williams was a beefy former detective who also had a degree in accounting. He was book smart, not street smart and he was real good about some kinds of crime and with some clients. Freddy was slightly dumpy and no one would ever guess he was a security man. He also liked management, keeping books and running the office. That was a blessing for me. I have no interest in business stuff at all. Freddy said he wasn't gay, he just liked sex with men. I never went into that at all.

Virgil Goodhue was a former football player who just got along with just about everybody. He was big, blond, crew cut and clean cut. He kind of inspired confidence in our clients. He was a nice guy to have around the house, or at a party. Butch said when the clients saw me, they went to hide their daughters. Virgil didn't have that problem.

The City Police approach to safety got to be downright odd. They cut salaries and forbid moonlight work and off hours working. They said you needed eight hours of sleep, or you weren't fresh enough, you weren't giving your all to the City. They also didn't believe "unworthy organizations" deserved protection. The "unworthy" included topless clubs, gay bars, and women's medical clinics.

We soon got calls from Planned Parenthood and from Beth Israel, a big temple in downtown. The City said they didn't provide protection for churches, thus they wouldn't protect the temple. It turned out the Center for Women and the Temple were in the same block. It was a formula for trouble. Adding to the brew was the office of Richmond Times, a gay newspaper. It was across the street from the Temple.

You wouldn't think that the anti-abortion people would be worried about the gays. Lesbian and gay couples don't need abortions, or birth control for that matter. You would be wrong. The Temple was protected by Inland Security, one of our best clients. They saw trouble coming and gave us a call. Officially, Inland protected the Temple. We provided the beef.

The Center for Women had Richmond Security. It was essentially a night watchman service. They hired a number of nice retired guys. They wore uniforms and hoped the uniform would scare away the bad guys. Every Friday, Virgil and I made it a point to prowl the area around the Temple, keeping an eye on the Women's Center too. There had been several fire bombings of the clinic in the past.

I wish I could say I anticipated the disaster. I knew there were potential problems and I was uneasy. I hadn't guessed it would be a truck bomb.

I was the first to see it. When you watch a street, you know the usual traffic. Every street has a pattern. This van drove up. It said it was the Wythville Automotive Supply Company. Wythville is the other side of the state. It just parked next to the drop off space for the Temple and two guys got out and walked away from it. They weren't automotive parts kind of guys. I know what those guys look like. The van had paper taped to the windows so you couldn't see in. It was brand new paper, not stained and dirty like any respectable van.

It was the middle of the month and Friday, about three in the afternoon. I called Butch and he said to call the Police. They said it was all right to park. I told them it was nosed into the drop off lane and should be towed. They did nothing.

I called Butch again. He said he would bring Roger over. I was afraid I was making a mountain over a molehill, but I managed to convince myself that the usual number of demonstrators at the Woman's building weren't there. That meant something. By now it was almost five and Sabbath Services would start shortly.

No one harassed the employees and Doctors at the Women's Center as they began to leave for the night. I was getting really worried. Virgil talked to Rabbi Cohen and the Director of the Woman's Center. They were concerned. At 5:30, Butch arrived with Roger. Roger is a retired police dog. Roger was a sniffer. He had bad arthritis, but his mind and nose were still good.

Roger went bonkers. He had found the mother load.

"Holy Shit!" Butch said. I already had dialed 911 and told them we had a bomb. They came that time. The Fire Department beat the Police to the site by five minutes. The ATF men arrived too. There were ten or twenty people in the Temple getting ready for services and over a hundred kids in its Hebrew School. Butch called our office which was only a few blocks away and we sent people to warn the residents of the apartment houses to leave.

The Fire Department was great. The patrolmen were great. The Chief of Police didn't show, nor did the Mayor. They said it was too dangerous.

I was kicking myself for knowing nothing about bombs. Muggers don't use bombs and I'm not much on watching the news. I had an idea that a lot of explosive could be packed in a van, but didn't really know. I went to the back of the Temple and found the school kids and their teachers lined up in the alley. This didn't seem far enough away, so I led them through the backyard of a house, into the next street. This was a real nice neighborhood and the yard was pretty,

The neighbors on the street were all looking panicked as they tried to collect their kids, cats and dogs and get away, but they were under control. A nice woman told us to go through her yard and off to the next street. This was a city neighborhood, so there was only three feet between the houses. This made moving the kids slow, but the solid mass of brick houses would provide some protection if there was a blast. Rabbi Cohen caught up with us and collapsed. He told me to take care of the the kids.

An Indian doctor wearing a turban appeared. He lived in the house whose yard we were crossing. He looked at the Rabbi and told us to move out quickly he would help Cohen. They were friends I guess. Cohen wanted me to take some bundles he had been carrying, so I did and we got to the next street. It was a mad house of fire engines, ambulances and people. I was afraid we would lose a kid.

A minister and several women saw us and told us to follow them. We walked another block and went into a big church. He took us to the basement and it was suddenly quiet. Everything will be fine, I thought. Then I heard a gigantic explosion. It was muffled, but I knew what it was. A few seconds later there were more explosions, like giant popcorn popping. I left the kids and teachers in the hands of the Minister and went out to the street.

There was glass everywhere. I looked down and realized it was broken stained glass windows. The windows on the upper floor of the church were blown out. Smoke was rising from the area near the Temple, so I ran back.

The smoke cleared for a minute and I saw every window in a high rise for the elderly was blown out. There was a big fire at the Temple, but smaller plumes of smoke began to rise from other buildings. I turned the corner and saw burning fire engines and an ambulance on fire in the middle of the street.

It looked as if there were bodies everywhere. Since I had been in the church during the explosion I was moving as if nothing had happened. Most of the guys in the street had been stunned, or were in shock from the blast. I didn't know if the people in the street were seriously hurt. Firemen and emergency people arrived from the side streets about when I did. Broken glass was the only problems for the people outside of the immediate blast area. That, and the fire of course.

I found Butch, he was cut, but not badly. He had lost Roger, but was helping a badly cut woman get to an ambulance. Virgil was at the Woman's center. It had been cleared completely, so no one was hurt there. He was with another one of our employees going into the apartment house next door.

The firemen seemed disorganized, so no one was telling you to stay away. There was a constant wail of ambulances, as additional fire equipment arrived. There was a burned out car in the middle of the street. It had the

Fire Chief's insignia on the unburned side. I had a bad feeling about that. I couldn't get near the Temple, so I went to the other side of the street and crossed through the back yards. The houses whose yards we had crossed to escape were burning. I almost felt sick thinking how close the kids had been to being burned.

I saw the turbaned Doctor giving first aid in the middle of the next street. There was blood everywhere. Broken glass almost looked like snow, or sleet on the street. The Police didn't have control of the situation, so the residents were fending for themselves. There were sheets, blankets and towels being used as bandages.

Elinor Salina was organizing 'Search and Rescue' parties. This was her street, she knew everyone there and was firmly in control. She also was used to command and very decisive. Everyone did what she told them to do.

"Clydesdale!" she cried. "No one has been in the elderly apartment house. Take Ben here and check it out." Ben was a college student. The University's Art building was at the end of the street and Ben looked like an artist type. Ben and some of his friends followed me and we went to the apartment. The apartment was a mess. All the windows on one side had been blown out and the residents were lost and in shock. I decided to get them out of the building and into the church where I had stashed the children. Ben had a cell phone and soon he seemed to get all the available art students pushing, carrying, or leading the elderly residents to safety. It was easy to get the residents who were wandering in the halls. The rooms were another matter.

Some people were hiding in terror. Some rooms were... The right word doesn't exist to describe what we found.

The next two days were a blur. I don't really know what I did. Everyone did whatever was needed. I was no exception. I gave detailed statements to the Police and the Feds. My picture appeared on the front page of the paper leading the children to safety and carrying the Torah. I had no idea what was in the bundle. I looked like a cross between the Pied Piper and Moses. The local TV people knew who I was, but kept my name out of the news. They listed me as a local resident. I didn't want any publicity. I wanted to catch some bombers.

In the end, twenty three people died, twelve firemen, two police, three ATF agents and the rest were residents. Two of the residents were in the apartment house I searched. 674 people were wounded, mostly with cuts, some were real bad. I felt good only two were killed in the apartment house. If you had seen what is was like, you wouldn't have thought anyone could have survived the shattered glass.

Our office and my apartment became the headquarters of several rescue groups. As former policemen, we had connections to a number of the rescue units that came to help. They crashed at my place. A shower and an hour of sleep was a godsend to many of the men. Ari organized the local restaurants and they provided food. The gay bar, three blocks away from the site, served as a cafeteria.

I would get home at three in the morning and find three guys sleeping in my room and two in the shower. I'd take a shower and sleep in a chair. Someone from Ari's restaurant would arrive with sandwiches and snacks.

We organized the protection of the damaged buildings and houses. The City Police seemed to be uninterested in looting. The Mayor didn't ask for additional state help. Fortunately there were a number of retired policemen who were eager to work for us. We were able to do what we promised to do. My friend John and his company, Millennium Construction, organized the stabilization of the damaged buildings. He was real organized.

A week later I sat down with Butch. We were going to have two guys spending the night. They were from the East Zion Crossroads Rescue Squad who had to wait to take someone home the next day. Just about every rescue squad within 100 miles helped.

"How is Roger?" I asked. I had completely forgotten about the dog.

"Dead. He was killed in the blast." Butch said. I started to cry. I couldn't believe it. I was crying over the dog. Butch put his arm around me. We weren't affectionate even though we had sex many times. It felt good.

"Roger was a happy dog. He had found the mother load. It was the best day of his life. He was old and in pain and as the last thing he did, he saved hundreds of people's lives," Butch said. I don't think I was crying about the dog only. It was all the people whose lives had been ruined or changed. I just got sort of overwhelmed. For a moment, it was too much for me. We talked for awhile and I felt better.

"I need to get to bed," I said finally.

"You can't. We've got company," Butch said. I had forgotten about the men. They hadn't arrived yet, but were due any minute.

"I'll sleep on the couch," I said. Butch looked at me a bit sheepishly.

"I kind of promised them some fun," he said. "Sandy, the paramedic is an old friend of mine. We were playmates once. He and a friend of his were hoping for some serious relaxation time."

"Shit!" I said. "I was hoping for some sleep." I was really annoyed. "Is he a bottom?" I asked without thinking. I hadn't thought about sex in a week.

"The best bottom I've ever known," Butch said. "He loves it and never gets tired. He can go as long as you can." The doorbell rang. I really wasn't interested in having sex with two strangers. Until I saw them.

They had the afternoon off and had gone to the site to help clear rubble. They were working in one of the burned houses. The two men were totally covered in soot and grime. Butch made them strip at the door and he took their clothes to the washer. I took them to the shower. I kind of like guys who work hard and these boys were my type. I really didn't have much idea what they looked like. Soot gets into everything, so their bodies were as black as their clothes. We all got in the shower and scrubbed them down.

Sandy was a big blond guy with a close cropped beard and blue eyes. He was tanned and covered in short blond hair from his neck to his toes. He had classic bear balls and cock, compact and rounded. Mark, his partner, was tall, maybe 6'-4" and ungainly. He had a handlebar mustache and a thick covering of hair on his chest and gut. He seemed to be built a bit like Goofy, nothing seemed to be attached right. Except for his cock. It was a prize winner. I've got a big one, but his was bigger.

Sandy was an old friend of Butch, but it only took three or four minutes to realize they were current friends too. Sure, Butch got his cock in Sandy's hole in record time, but they weren't fucking. Butch and Sandy were making love. As I said before, Butch wasn't normally an affectionate kind of guy, but I think the bombing must have changed him some.

I looked at Mark and he looked at me and we knew we were going to have a good night. Ugly guys with great cocks have a problem. Lots of people get turned on by big cocks and they like them. But you can't just walk around town waving your cock at passers by. Once I'm naked, I do pretty well. It may not be love, but I don't mind satisfying a guy's curiosity, if it means he'll drain my balls. Mark and I both had an asset we couldn't market. We understood each other. We were soul mates.

Mark was 6'4 and I am 5'4' and remarkably everything fit. We sixty-nined and it was as if our tonsils had been waiting our entire life to be touched by the other man's cock. He oozed real cock jam. I could work my tongue deep into his piss slit and taste it newly minted. I've never been a fancier of cock juice, neither precum nor cum. It was always a sign of a job well done to me, but not the main attraction. Somehow, Mark's cock dribble really hit the spot. It was sweet. I told him that and he said, it was "Redneck Surprise" flavor and he made it specially for me.

Mark and I weren't making love. It was sex, pure and simple. Maybe not that pure, come to think of it. Sometimes the sex is so good it becomes something else. That was Mark and me. We spent half the night draining each other's cocks, then I slipped my meat into his love tunnel and he liked it more than I did. That is saying a lot. My cock felt like it was home at last.

It went in easy, then Mark tightened his chute. It felt as if his ass was shrink wrapped to my cock. I would thrust and then pull back and he tried to hold it, as if his ass didn't want my cock to leave. I don't know how long we fucked, but it was great. I woke the next morning with his cock a few inches from my mouth. We fell asleep in the 69 position. He rotated and whispered to me.

"Your back door unlocked?" he asked. "I've been dreaming about it all night." I'm not much of a bottom, but I didn't want to disappoint.

"You're big," I said. His meat was bigger than mine. He had a huge head on a long shaft, it was like a lollipop. I've got a club cock with the head the same size as the shaft. I wasn't too enthusiastic. Mark must have felt my hesitation. He felt my ass. He had lubed his finger and I opened up some. Usually I tense up when someone touches my hole. Not this time.

"I know it's big. Once the head is in, they tell me it's really relaxing," said Mark. His fingers were real long and he poked my prostate and I couldn't breath for a second. I was going to say I wasn't real sure about this but the pressure on my prostate was too much for me to talk. "I'll ram the head through real fast. You hardly notice," he said.

Somehow he got my legs on his shoulder and my ass open wide. He did what he said he would. There was a sharp pain, then his pubic hair was touching my ass. I didn't know what to feel. He moaned.

"Shit! It's going to be hard not to shoot!" he said. Mark was wrong about that. The boy had good control. He began to pull out again, withdrawing three or four inches, then he reversed course. He did this a few times and I began to warm up. His shaft wasn't really thin, it was just thin compared to the head. As he fucked, the shaft seemed to disappear and I only felt the head moving in my love tunnel. It felt okay after a few thrusts, kind of good after a few more and then I lost it.

I like to be in control, but I felt an avalanche of feeling. Waves of sensation flowed over me and through me. I came, but he didn't stop and I didn't mind. He came a minute or two later and I had a second orgasm. Butch later told me my cock looked like a fountain of cum spraying my sperm all over the room.

Mark pulled out and I felt empty. Butch came over and replaced him in my ass. He had never fucked me before.

"You looked like you need a soft landing, little buddy," he said. His cock felt good too, not as intense as with Mark, but real nice. My cock was still drooling cum. Butch pulled back, so only the head was in my ass. "If I do this much longer I'm going to shoot," he said

"Go for it," I replied. I will swear I could feel the cum spurting from his cock. It was that good.

Part 3

Mark and Sandy had to go that morning. For all practical purposes they were running a medical taxi service between Richmond and the Medical Center in Charlottesville, so they were around a lot. That was fine for me.

After the explosion I learned a lot about myself and the people around me. Disasters bring out the best in most people. If you aren't destroyed by it, you will get stronger. Most people pass the test. Only a few fail. Nobody at Clydesdale & Company failed. I was proud of that.

The bombing was a coward's way to fight, a surprise attack on the unsuspecting and the innocent. The explosion took place at a Jewish Synagogue, across the street from a gay newspaper and a Woman's Heath Clinic. The situation was like one of those old murder mysteries where there are too many suspects and too many motives.

The Police seemed to think it was an old fashioned, Anti-Semitic group. My guess was an anti-abortion group. They liked violence and I figured, if they killed some Jews or Gays in the process, they wouldn't be too worried. I knew the Mayor and the Police Chief were in bed with the born agains and had ties to the anti-abortion groups. They said they weren't, but I know a weasel-like liar when I see one. The Mayor made me want to puke.

The Police Chief assigned Captain Walker to the case. He was a nice man who was nearing retirement and had specialized in domestic violence cases. He had zero experience with this sort of case and no energy. The Fire Department was in disarray since the Chief had been killed in the explosion and the Mayor decided to have a nationwide search to find a replacement. He appointed a bookkeeper as interim head of the department until a new Chief could be selected.

We had some of the best minds from Police Department working for us. Butch never said it, but we all wanted to catch the bombers and I guessed we had as good a chance as anybody. We knew Richmond real well. I was only real eyewitnesses of the truck and the men who drove it. I hadn't seen much, but I had seen more than anyone else. I had a special reason for wanting to catch the guys.

I had nightmares about the terrified children racing through the backyards of houses and then of the elderly people sliced to pieces in their apartments. We kept on running, but could never get ahead of the glass daggers.

As the good guys, we were supposed to play by the rules. I believe in the rules, but I don't mind stretching and bending them a bit for a good cause. They say that revenge isn't noble, but I am not a very noble guy. I wanted to get the bombers and make them pay. I wasn't thinking of prison for the rest of their lives, or even a nice sanitary lethal injection. I was thinking of something more personal. I didn't know exactly what this would be, but I got a warm feeling of satisfaction just thinking about it. That helped with the nightmares.

I was explaining my plans to catch the bombers to John and his friend Billy at lunch. We were in John's house and I needed John's advice. I tend to be a doer, not a thinker. John was good at thinking. My big problem was information. I had my own, but I couldn't get the official stuff. John had the same misgivings about the Mayor.

"I don't think he had anything to do with the bombing, mind you," John said, "but he's in bed with those guys. He's afraid if it turns out to be them, he's dead meat."

"The Mayor's scared shitless," Billy said. "He's in way over his head and is afraid to come clean. He's afraid to look under the rocks and will do anything he can to keep the Police off the trail."

"I think there is a solution for your information problem," John said. "My guys are working on the site every day. They hear a lot." The Millennium Construction Company was stabilizing the buildings and were removing the parts of the buildings too badly damaged to be saved. He had a great group of guys working for him. "We hear everything that is said by the investigators. Vince DeSoto is associated with the Fire Department's investigation. Ram is part of the State Task Force doing psychological profiles."

"Damn!" Billy said.

"Damn what?" John asked.

"Do you realize with Clydesdale, Vince and Ram, we have the guys with the biggest cocks in the city working on the investigation," We all burst out laughing. "Horse Hung & Company, Private Dicks!"

"Horse Hung & Company, Professional Dicks!" I said. "It sure is convenient. They're all smart guys. The combination of intelligence and cock is sure attractive. I'd been too busy for sex, but I gave it a trial run a week ago, just to make sure everything still worked."

"Did it?" Billy asked.

"Yes Sir!" I replied. "With the bombing and all the dead and wounded, it didn't seem right to be thinking about sex. Damn if I didn't feel a lot better when I got my cock in a rescue worker's ass. And I do mean a lot better!"

"I thought you always feel good when you are fucking!" John said. He had a point. The doorbell rang. John went to get it. I could hear a man with a country accent ask if I was there. Moments later Mark entered with John.

"Sorry to bother you, but Butch said you were here," Mark said. "I'm only free for a few hours." I introduced him to John and Billy.

"We were just talking about you," I said. "I was recommending 'red neck" sex for tension relief. I was saying how good it was the other night."

"It works for me," he said without batting a eye, "I take it you guys are members of the fraternity?"

"John here is the Pledge Master," Billy said, smiling.

"How do I join?"

"I think Clydesdale may have already filled out your papers," John said. Mark bellowed in laughter.

"That's what he was doing in my ass!" he said. "I thought it took a lot more time than a plain old fuck!"

"Damn, Clydesdale! You attract the strong silent types," Billy said. "Shy and a looker too." Mark was wearing his EMT uniform with the white shirt unbuttoned almost to his navel. He puffed out his chest and fluffed up the hair on is chest.

"Your friends are real perceptive, Clydesdale," Mark said. "I'm the guy for guys who like manly men! Lots of kids can't recognize a real man when they see one."

"You like kids?" Billy asked.

"Hell, I been fucking with Clydesdale!" Mark replied. "He ain't no kid and he ain't no movie star. I'm even beginning to have serious doubts about his virginity. He told me it really wasn't sex. It was therapy!"

"I think of it as therapy too," Billy said. "I do therapy for a living but a good ride on a cock can do wonders."

"Are you serious?" asked John. "I don't seem to remember reading that in Time or Newsweek as a recent breakthrough."

"Actually I do think it is true," Billy said. By the expression on his face I could tell that he had just thought of that. "An orgasm is as good as things get from a physical point of view. It's good to get the juices flowing for something other than the disaster."

"You have a point there," John said. "I've been eating, drinking and sleeping the bomb site for two weeks. You need a break after a while." Mark looked at me and then John and Billy. I think the same idea struck us at the same time. I knew he didn't mind screwing in a group, but I wasn't sure he was with the program until I looked at his pants. They were tight and you could tell he was interested.

"Anyone for group therapy?" Billy asked. Everyone laughed.

"Sounds good to me!" Mark said. "I don't know you guys, but I'm game if you are. I'm not a real refined kind of guy and I kind of have my heart set on a good fucking. I like sucking too, mind you, but I really want some ass action."

"Truthfully Mark, you've got nothing to worry about," I said. "Everyone is ambidextrous!" We wandered off to John's bedroom. Skeeter came in. He lived in John's attic and was a spectacular cum hound. He assumed he was welcome to join us. He was right.

Billy and Mark were almost naked by the time we got to the bedroom. Billy was a short, beefy hair ball. He was my height, but had a good 60 pounds on me. He and Mark hit it off. Mark had a special skill in 69ing with guys a foot shorter than himself.

Billy had almost no cock at all when he was soft, but he had a long and thin one hard. It vanished effortlessly in Mark's throat. Mark's donkey dong was a different challenge for Billy. Billy was willing, but there was just too much. Skeeter joined in to resolve the dilemma. It was almost too big for Skeeter, but, as always, Skeeter rose to the occasion.

I was feeling like a little play time with Mark, but slipped into John's ass for old time's sake. Automatic pilot took over and I have to admit it was as good as it ever got. We hadn't fucked in three weeks and we were overdue. I was enjoying myself royally when I felt something at my back door. It was Mark and his cock.

He bent me forward and rammed my ass. As before, he popped the cock head through the hole before he buried the next ten inches in my ass. One of those strange feelings overwhelmed me and I started to kiss John. The added force of Mark ramming my ass seemed to drive me deeper into John and we both could feel it.

Ramming is the wrong word. Mark was a goofy looking guy and no brighter than he needed to be. He had said once he had a second brain in his cock for use in emergencies. After three or four exploratory thrusts, he began to adjust and shift to maximize the sensation. I knew then what he meant. The brain in his cock was directing us all. Pretty soon we were a single mass of cock, ass and hair, all quivering in ecstasy.

John shot first. He moaned and I could feel the warm sticky cum squirting between us. His ass contracted. That was enough for me. I shot and had passed the high point of my ejaculations when Mark let out a rebel yell. He was a rough fucker as he ejaculated, but I was so relaxed by then I didn't care. Actually I did. I had a second orgasm, almost as strong as the first. We all collapsed in a pile.

"I didn't know you took it in the ass?" John whispered.

"I didn't know myself until last week," I said.

"It's a nice addition," John said. Damn if I didn't kiss him again. His ass spasmed and I had another ejaculation. Mark was still in my ass and gave me another few thrusts. I was sure the last drops of seed oozed from his cock. We broke apart and Skeeter wormed his way in and cleaned the cum from John's gut. Billy was almost asleep, but I didn't know if that was the result of Skeeter or Mark's efforts. Mark had to leave to get back to work.

"Damn, I feel good," John exclaimed. "Billy, I think there may be something to your theory that sex helps reduce stress."

"I know it helps me!" I said.

"It of course reduces sexual tension, but I think it helps with plain old garden variety stress," Billy said.

"I haven't thought about sex in the last three weeks," John said. "I'm just glad it helps with stress induced by a mad bomber." We all laughed. I had to admit I was feeling good. I had to get to work and wasn't even dreading it. It was a good day.

I was patrolling the bombed area with Roosevelt. One side of the temple was blown out, but the dome stood, supported by the other walls. The John's men were finishing up a scaffold that braced the dome and held the remaining walls in place. I talked to the superintendent, Tom. He had a crew which had been working on another project on the Bay. They were brought in to help with the emergency work. Bubba and a guy named Wayne were jacking bracing into place.

Otto and Lance, John's swishy painters were working on the inside of the temple. They were trying to save the interior paintings. When I first saw the damage I didn't think any thing could be saved, but they had worked miracles. Some of the art students who had gone to the elderly apartment house with me were working with Otto. I never much took to Otto. He wasn't my type, but he knew his stuff and knew how to work. Plywood and blue tarps were beginning to close up the building.

It was a beautiful building and it seemed indecent to have its interior exposed to view. I was relieved to see the tarps. The school next door was leveled. That was no loss, but I still got a little sick to my stomach every time I thought of what might have happened.

A block away, I saw some guys who didn't belong on the street. I've got a nose for bad actors. Roosevelt is good about black guys. He can tell trash from real folk. I can tell construction workers, rescue volunteers from trailer trash. I trailed them as Roosevelt called in for back up. I had guessed right. The city cop arrived, searched them and struck gold, real gold. They had been steeling jewelry from the damaged houses.

Eleanor arrived and she could identify some of the pieces. These city neighborhoods were really close and she remembered a necklace worn by a neighbor at a Christmas party. One guy tried to make a break for it. I got him. Somehow he broke his leg as I tackled him. It was a good day.

I got home at seven and had a call to go to John's for dinner and to bring any of my group along with me. Butch and Freddy came along. Virgil and Roosevelt held the fort.

We got there at 7:30 and Vince, the fireman and Ram, the psychiatrist, were there, as were two guys I hadn't met before, Julio and Steve. They were out of town arson investigators. Tom and another new guy, Trent were also there. They were the job superintendents for the emergency work at the bomb site. John's neighbors were also there. Larry was an artist but had his laptop and was taking notes. His other neighbors provided the food. Eleanor, the civic leader and Earnest Waldburg arrived just after we did. Waldburg was the President of the Temple.

John ran things. I knew him as a friend and as a sex partner, but not as a businessman. He ran a big company and he was organized and in control. Vince gave a report. He said that the interim Fire Chief wasn't with the Mayor's program. He was a bean counter, but was deeply offended and enraged at the bombing. "He took it really personally. He told me to get the best men I could get and catch them," Vince said. "The cops feel the same way, it's leadership they lack. No co-ordination by the top brass." Julio then gave a quick overview of the preliminary information.

The device was simple and made up of materials you could buy at a Lowe's or Home Depot. The van was stolen. Most interesting were the timers. One was set for 5:00, the other was to go at 5:45. The van blew up at 5:43. Apparently the one clock malfunctioned and the other was fast.

I explained the schedules of the organizations in the area. 5:00 was the time the Woman's Health Center closed and the quitting time for the Gay newspaper. The Hebrew school normally ended at 4:00 but there was a special program the Friday of the explosion. The services were normally at 7:00. The second timer meant that the bomber was trying to kill rescuers. If the first bomb went of at 5:00 the site would have been filled with people trying to help the wounded.

My guess was the bombing was aimed at the Women's Clinic not the temple. This seemed to confirmed that guess. The small popcorn like explosions were gasoline containers that had been made into mini bombs. They blew out of the Van with the big explosions and then blew up in the air. The van was to destroy a specific place, the mini bombs couldn't be aimed. They were to confuse the situation with random explosions.

"The device is simple but deadly," Steve said. "I don't know why the bombers were after the rescue workers? They have nothing to do with the Women's Clinic or the Temple for that matter."

"Authority figures," Ram said. "And agents of the government. You think of Firemen and Police as public servants. The bombers see them as Agents of the Government."

"The bomb has some Middle Eastern characteristics. The effort to kill rescue workers is typical," Waldburg said. "But, they have their own supply of high powered explosives, so they wouldn't need to use homemade ingredients. I called the Israeli Embassy in Washington. They don't think it's a Palestinian or Arab who did it. They know the modus operandi of those groups well. They think it's local."

"I assume they are checking it carefully?" Vince asked.

"Oh yes," he answered. "With typical Jewish thoroughness, I might add. We too are worried about the Police Departments sincerity. We have set up a reward of $250,000.00 for the bombers capture. We have a check for $100,000.00 for Clydesdale & Company for saving the children."

"We don't take rewards. It's our job," Butch said. "But that money could broaden our investigation. Let's think of it as a retainer."

"Just remember that cash is not a problem," Eleanor said. "If you need more just come to Earnest or me. There are deep pockets willing to do what it takes to get these guys."

The meeting had gotten off to a good start. We had a plan. We had pooled our resources. Clydesdale and Co. was to do the field work at the site. Freddy was going to do an Internet search, hunting for clues on the net. I didn't know what he was planning exactly, but he seemed sure he would find something.

The meeting broke up at 11:00. It had been a good day. I got a call the next morning telling me my Uncle Jake had died. He was a nice guy and my Mom was real distressed. I had to go to the funeral. I was out of town for three days.

Jake had been real important to me when I was a teenager. I always like guys more than girls and I seemed to think that was bad. I also tried drinking a lot and be a macho asshole. Somehow I thought this would make me a man and not a fag. Jake taught me how to like men and be a man at the same time.

He also taught me how to enjoy sex. Quick and fast had been my approach to sex. I thought if you had a quick blow job, if it was fast enough, it might not be sex and I might not be gay. He was real big, liked hunting and fishing and seemed like a real man and loved sex with real men. I didn't know you could do all of it.

He wasn't into young guys, but he did show me the ropes. He liked older men, but my cock saved the day for me. I learned the advantages of being donkey dicked from him. Jake liked them big and curiosity got the better of him. Once I got naked and hard, guys tended to make exceptions for me.

Mom was glad to see me and I was a local hero. My picture had been in the local papers so everyone was nice to me. That included some people who had been uppity before. My cousin, Buddy was real nice too. He and I had the same training program with Uncle Jake. Buddy was ten years older than me and had a wife and three kids. Buddy and his wife were on the outs. He didn't seem to know why. I could guess. He asked me to stop by his farm on my way back to Richmond. I said I would.

The day after the funeral I left early so I could be back to Richmond by the afternoon. The drive from deepest south-west Virginia is a long one. I almost forgot about stopping at Buddy's, but I remembered as I drove by.

It was his Daddy's farm and Buddy kept it up well. The fences were in good shape as was the house. Buddy heard me drive in and asked me into the kitchen for some breakfast. He told me his tale of woe. Sally, his wife had left him. She had found God with a vengeance and Buddy wasn't virtuous enough for her. She knew nothing about his liking for cock. It was milking the cows that did him in. Milking on Sundays.

"You'll kill the fucking cow if you don't milk 'em!" Buddy said in exasperation. I knew he was bothered. He was a good Southern Baptist type cock sucker. He didn't drink, or smoke, or swear normally. A liking for cock was his only vice and that he did only in moderation.

"I was wondering why she wasn't at the funeral," I said. "Folks go to funerals even if there's been a divorce. It's expected."

"I told her. It reflects badly," Buddy said. "She wanted to keep the kids away from bad influences. She doesn't hold with even entering "false" churches. She's worried she'll get contaminated."

"By the Presbyterians?"

"Yep, that's her worry. I told her you'd be there," Buddy continued. "She used to like you. She said you were working for the baby killers. The preacher man she likes said the bombing was God's judgment on evil. When she saw you in the paper, she said you were interfering with God's will."

"Damn. She is over the top," I said. "What's the name of her preacher man? I might like to have a nice sit down with him." A pick up drove up and interrupted our conversation. It was Sheriff Earl Evans. He was an old friend of Buddy's.

"How's it going?" he asked as he came to the door. The Sheriff looked at me. "You're the guy in the paper, aren't you?"

"Earl, this is my cousin, Clydesdale Noland," Buddy introduced us. We shook hands.

"Buddy's told me about you. It was a brave thing you did. I can't believe that sort of thing can happen here in Virginia. It's awful," the Sheriff said. "Do you have some leads?"

"Too early for that, but I'm afraid it may be something homegrown," I said.

"I'm afraid you may be right. I wouldn't have thought it was possible a few years ago. I'm not so sure now. There are more nut cases out there than I want to admit."

"Buddy was telling me about his wife," I said.

"That's my point exactly," the Sheriff agreed. "Sally needs help, not God. That group she belongs to is a sick one." The phone rang and Buddy left the room to answer it. The Sheriff got closer to me. "Are you the cousin Buddy said is hung like Trigger?"

"I don't rightly know," I said. "He might have a better hung cousin. I kind of doubt it, though. " The Sheriff felt my crotch.

"I think you're the one. Buddy and I are playmates sometimes. I like them big and Buddy said I'd like you," he said. "Your Uncle was a good friend of mine. He said you were a good boy." Buddy entered the room.

"You guys seem to have broken the ice!" he said smiling. "Clydesdale. Earl has been coming by from time to time to cheer me up, what with Sally gone." Sheriff Evans wore a wedding ring, so I guessed a playmate with a place of his own and no wife in residence was a powerful attraction.

"I was telling Clydesdale your Uncle taught me a lot," Earl said. "I'm a lot more open minded than I was. I'm going to miss him."

"If Uncle Jake was here now we'd all be naked and enjoying ourselves," I said. The Sheriff looked at me with a twinkle in his eye.

"How about a memorial orgasm for the old fucker?" he said.

"That is a plan!" Buddy said. "Let's go upstairs to the bedroom."

Part 4

My romp with Buddy and the Sheriff turned out to be fun. Buddy was a careful sucker. He loved to be sucked and sucked you only to be polite. I'm not sure he thought it really was sex. He had been doing it since he was a kid and it was purely recreational for him. He wasn't emotionally involved.

Don't get me wrong. He was really appreciative and liked it a lot. He enjoyed it, so a good time was had by all. It was like a good massage for him, except his cock was being massaged. The Sheriff, Earl, was completely different.

I had never had sex with him and it took me a good minute and a half to realize he loved cock and sex with men. He liked it and wasn't ashamed to like it. He got on his knees sucking me and Buddy in a split second. He also had a finger searching out my hole too. Buddy was 6-2 and 250 pounds with a dusting of red hair on his chest. He had what Uncle Jake referred to as a good recreational cock. It tasted good and didn't choke you.

Earl was a lot like Butch, but older and a bit heavier. Unlike Butch, Earl wasn't the strong silent type. He liked sex and wasn't afraid if you knew it. His finger poked a real nice spot in my ass.

"You like that, Clydesdale?" he asked.

"I sure do!" I said. "This ain't your first time in a guy's ass, is it?"

"Shit no," he replied. "I've had some quality time working with a guy's bells and whistles. You know, every guy's ass is different, though. You're an open book. Everything's where it should be and in working condition. It took me a long time to find Buddy's 'on' button!" With that comment he switched to sucking Buddy. Much to my surprise, he was fingering Buddy. Buddy's hole had been off limits when we were kids. Buddy was rolling his eyes back as Earl's finger hit a good spot. I leaned over and sucked one of Buddy's big pink nipples. Buddy moaned in pleasure.

"He liked that, suck them harder!" Earl said. I did. Buddy moaned again.

"Stop!" Buddy cried. "I going to shoot. Hold up some! I don't want to shoot too soon," Earl stopped sucking.

"You into fucking, Clydesdale?" the Sheriff asked.

"I sure am! I love it," I said. "But, I'm kind of partial to the top. Not always, mind you. Just a preference."

"This is your lucky day, Clydesdale," Earl said. "I haven't had a cock like yours in my ass in years. Not since Elmer Williams left town."

"Shit, I'd forgotten about Elmer. You got his whole monster in your ass?" I asked. Elmer was the football coach at the high school.

"I think your meat is just as big," Earl said. "Elmer was great." He paused. "Buddy, do you mind if Clydesdale and I get a bit up close and personal?"

"No, go right ahead," Buddy said. He was uncomfortable. "I don't want to do it myself," he added a bit uncertainly.

"Great, you wouldn't mind watching would you?" Earl asked.

"Actually, I think I'm kind of interested," Buddy said. "I've never seen guys fuck."

"Do you have some lube?" Earl asked. He stroked my cock. "I'm not going to take that donkey dong dry!" Buddy had some Cornhuskers and that did the trick. I asked Earl how he wanted it, spread eagle or doggy style. He said he liked it spread eagle, if I could take it easy at the start.

"That's no problem for me, as long as you don't mind it a bit more intense near the end," I said. Earl smiled.

"I wouldn't have it any other way, at the end," he said. Earl got on the bed and laid back. I got his legs on my shoulders. The bed was low and my cock was at perfect ass hole height. My cock was coated in Cornhuskers. His pink ass winked at me and had a little rosebud poking out of the opening. I pulled my skin back a little, so the piss slit lined up exactly with the rosebud and rested the head at his hole. I applied a little pressure. I wasn't pushing, just letting him know I was ready.

He had been nice and hard before. As soon as he felt the head at his ass, his cock doubled in size. His cock head was so bloated that it was shinny. I could see my refection in it. I squirted some Cornhuskers on his cock and stroked it. On the third stroke I pushed my cock forward. He opened up like the Red Sea did for Moses. My cock head slipped in and Earl moaned.

I didn't want to overdo the first thrust. I rested it there and then pulled out. After adding some more lube, I popped in again. Earl was real appreciative.

"Is the whole thing going to fit?" Buddy asked. I looked at my cock. I had noticed Earl was real excited, but my own cock was looking pretty good too. I pushed four or five inches into Earl's ass.

"Believe me, it's all going to fit," I said. Buddy was looking good by now, hard and drooling precum. He was real excited. He was on his knees beside Earl on the bed. Earl had a finger or two in Buddy's ass. I thought it was nice of Earl to think of Buddy while he was being fucked. Earl was a real nice guy.

Earl's eyes suddenly glazed. I was fully embedded and Earl was a happy guy. We had a nice slow fuck for a while. He asked me to pull out so he could rest a little before we finished up. I pulled out and cooled down some. It was real nice. I looked over at Buddy and could tell he wanted to fuck too, but was too embarrassed to ask. I looked at Earl and he had noticed the same thing.

"Come on, Buddy," Earl said. "Try it out and see if you like it!" Buddy jumped up and buried his cock in Earl's ass. Earl liked that too. Buddy sure was a fast learner.

"Damn, I'm going to shoot!" Buddy cried.

"Just leave it in and fill me up!" Earl said. "Your cousin, Clydesdale, won't mind your cum in my ass." Earl was right about that. I held Buddy so he couldn't pull out. Buddy had a four-alarm orgasm. I had seen him shoot many times over the years, but this was a prize winner. He shook and shuddered every time he shot. When he pulled out, I returned. You don't get to fuck a cum filled ass often and this was a real pleasure.

We had all played with Uncle Jake and this seemed like a fitting send off. I had to admit I liked Buddy's cum and the way it coated my cock when I pulled it out. It squeezed out between Earl's ass and my cock. Earl was a great bottom, he enjoyed it and would squeeze my cock with his ass to get me harder.

He began to shoot hands free. I came as his ass convulsed with his orgasm. He wouldn't let me pull out until I was completely soft. He said I had more cock soft than some men did hard. We all showered and got dressed. I had to get back to Richmond. Buddy looked a little lost.

"Are you okay, Buddy?" I asked.

"Yes, it was real good. I don't believe I did it," he said. "I don't believe I liked it so much either. I feel kind of dizzy."

"I was kind of hoping you would like it and give me a ride again," Earl said. He put his arm around Buddy's shoulder. "I don't mind helping out a friend and I can't tell you how much I enjoyed this morning." I knew the Sheriff liked my cock, but I had the feeling he really liked Buddy as a friend, not just a cock.

"I need to get going," I said. "If you guys would like to do some checking on our preacher man, I'd really appreciate it. I'd like to know more about him and his associates."

"I have some thoughts along that line too. Something isn't kosher there," the Sheriff said. "The difference between wacky and criminal is hard to tell sometimes. I've got some contacts in the group. They were thinking about getting out of it, but I asked them to stay an keep an eye open. The Preacher is getting stranger and stranger. You don't know what he might do next."

The Sheriff walked me to my car as Buddy went off to feed the animals.

"Thanks," he said. "You got one hell of a cock. It was everything Buddy said it was."

"Thanks for helping Buddy out. He's kind of lost with Sally and the kids gone," Earl laughed.

"He's a nice guy, you got him to loosen up. I've been trying to get him in my ass for years," Earl said. "We cock suckers need to stick together!" I drove away. I got back in late afternoon and went through the office messages. There was nothing that had to be done immediately. Ram and Billy dropped by. They had been working on a psychological profile of the bomber. They had proposed three scenarios, anti-Semitic, anti-abortion and anti-gay and were developing a profile for each.

The Police Force was looking into the anti-Semitic option, with emphasis on foreign terrorists. This seemed unlikely to me, but Ram said the Police Chief believed it and was doing a thorough job investigating it.

"We don't need to look there," Ram said. "It's covered. There is no work being done on the anti-abortion, or anti gay angle."

"I have the gay angle under control," Billy said. "Half the paranoid gays in town come to me for counseling. They aren't convinced. There weren't enough gays at the newspaper to justify the bomb. The chances that the editor or much of the staff would be there on a Friday afternoon is poor. They think gays were collateral damage. A bonus to the bomber, but not the main attraction."

"The main victims, other than the firemen and police, were the elderly," I said. "No one thinks they were the intended victim."

"I figure the bomber is either so single minded he doesn't consider other damage, or perhaps someone from the country, who is used to seeing places in isolation," Ram said.

"The other option is a sadist," Billy said. "Someone who enjoys inflicting pain."

"The timing is so odd. Amateur night. It seems to me professionals wouldn't have had the problem with the timer," I said. "I've been thinking along the lines of a 'born again' gone bad. You know, one of those guys who gets so holy, he gets messages from God." I was thinking about Buddy, his wife and her preacher. She was so holy, she had to leave her husband. And I would bet a million dollars she went to heavy duty family values church.

"I've been thinking along the lines of a Holy Roller too. Someone who is so obsessed with abortion, or gays they can't see clearly," Ram said. As the conversation progressed we all were tending to think the same thing. It was someone who didn't see that killing some innocent people was a problem, if they were able to get at the real sinners.

"Well, if they are after gays, we're goners!" Billy said. "I don't think they'd recognize us as gays."

"Shit, they wouldn't recognize their Minister or half the choir as being gay," I said. "They're all confirmed bachelors waiting for the right woman." Billy laughed. "I do think there is something sinful about women who don't get married. Virginity is good until you get married, but if you don't you turn out to be a dried up old spinster."

Someone knocked at the door. It was Mark and Vince.

"How did you guys meet?" I asked.

"We didn't," Vince said. "We just arrived at the door at the same time." I introduced them. They joined in the conversation. Vince said the preliminary lab reports on the explosive indicated all the materials were made in the U.S.A. None were foreign.

"That's the good news," Vince said. "The bad news is there is nothing that couldn't be bought at a Radio Shack, Wall-Mart or Southern States. There is nothing exotic at all in the mix."

"Damn, I was hoping for something in Arabic or Chinese," I said. "Maybe a 'Property of the KGB' sticker."

"Perhaps a half price sale sticker from the Bombs R Us store in downtown Baghdad," Billy added.

It was getting late and I ordered out for Chinese. It was a good conversation. It focused my mind some. I asked Mark if he was in town with the ambulance. He said no, it was the weekend and he wondered if I was free. I told him I thought I could work him into my social calendar.

"Is this a meeting of Horse Hung & Company?" Mark asked.

"Horse Hung & Company?" Vince asked. "What are you talking about?" I filled him in on the joke of the week before.

"There is some big meat here," Billy said. Vince looked at Mark and then at Billy. Billy nodded. Vince had never met Mark before, but Mark was a big boy too. "The only problem is that you all are tops. I'm the only bottom here and I'm not sure I can handle you all."

"I'm a switch hitter in a pinch," Mark said. "Clydesdale is too, but he doesn't want anyone to know it."

"Thanks for keeping my confidence so well!" I said. I had been a confirmed top for so long, I was a bit embarrassed at guys finding out my interests had changed some.

"I love to top, but my cock's hard to fit," Ram said. "I can't casually fuck a guy. It's a big production.

"Lot's of men like the eye candy, but when it comes to lying back and opening up, they either lose their nerve, or claim I'm trying to split them in half," Vince said.

"I've had that happen, but I can take it," Mark said. "I won't say it'll be easy, but I bet I can do it and I bet Clydesdale can too."

"What in hell are you volunteering me for?" I said. I was a bit annoyed, but also a bit interested.

"Well we big guys are always the centers of attention, once we get naked, that is. I'd never been with a guys as well endowed as me before I chanced on Clydesdale a few weeks ago," Mark said. "It was damn good. I'd never been plugged by anything as big as Clydesdale and I loved it."

"You want to do it again?" Ram asked.

"I sure do. Let's do some testing of the limits. I try your cock on for size and you try mine," Mark suggested. "Have you had a big one in your ass?"

"It seems odd to be talking about this sort of stuff," Vince said.

"You mean it's time to do it?" Billy asked. Vince smiled.

"That's exactly what I mean," Vince said. "I've heard a lot about your Architectural Digest shower, Clydesdale. Can you give us a tour?" I could and did. I locked up the office area and we trooped upstairs. We were naked by the time we hit the showers. Mark got next to me as the other guys went into my bathroom.

"Clydesdale," Mark whispered. "Have you ever been fucked by a black guy?"

"Nope. But Ram is Indian, not black."

"He's close enough for me," he continued. "Would it bother you if you saw a black cock in my ass?"

"Shit no. No problem," I said.

"Thanks. I'd be sorely tempted. I have a powerful urge," Mark said. "I wouldn't want it to come between us." We went into the bathroom and Billy was on the floor sucking Vince and Ram.

Mark took one look at Vince and Ram. They were half erect. "Hot damn! Christmas has come early this year!"

Part 5

The play period with Vince and Ram was quite a bit more than I expected. I was used to being the biggest boy in the room. My experience with Mark was pretty easy. His cock and my ass fit perfectly. Vince and Ram were no easy meat. Oddly it was less comfortable and enjoyable, but much more sexual. I'd been fucking guys for years and they've been complaining. I noticed while they might complain, most came back for more.

I had always attributed this to insincerity. After Vince spent some time in my ass, I realized what they felt. I didn't really like it the first time, but I knew I would get him back in my ass. He touched something in my hole that hadn't been touched before. The physical contact between cock and ass did things to my brain that hadn't been done before. These feelings were so different from what I usually experienced I didn't know what to think about them.

Vince was straight up about his fucking technique. He would be slow and careful for a while, but he tended to get carried away as his balls filled. I understood that myself, since I tended to be single minded as an orgasm approached. You can't stop a train at full speed.

Billy lubed us up good. He must have used a complete tube of K-Y. Vince slowly pumped his cock in. The head was as big as Mark's. Mark popped his cock head through my ass and it was clear sailing as the rest of the shaft entered. Every inch was a battle for Vince. His shaft was just as big as the head. I asked him to go slow and he did.

"I can't believe that cock can fit," Billy said as he watched and encouraged us. "That cock is the size of your arm!"

Vince was thrusting rhythmically, going a bit deeper on each thrust. It was really uncomfortable. It wasn't like being split in half, but I sure knew why some guys might think that. Mark was hooting and hollering as Ram did him. I am more of a grit your teeth guy.

Vince must have been seven or eight inches in when I lost it. I couldn't fight Vince's relentless thrusts. I felt as if his cock occupied me. I belonged to his cock. I relaxed and the monster went deep. It winded me. Vince was administering CPR through my ass. I couldn't think and Vince did all the thinking anyone needed to do at the time.

He stopped and pulled out. It was quiet except for heavy breathing.

"Damn!" Mark said. "That was a trip!" I looked over and saw Ram's cock freed from Mark's ass. "Did you shoot?"

"No," Ram said. "It takes a long session for me to pop. I just thought you could use a breather."

"I was getting to the point of no return here," Vince said. "I figured Clydesdale wouldn't mind a rest period. I've never fucked a guy as small. I don't want to break him." Vince looked at me and smiled. "You're a trooper. We don't have to finish up, if you don't want to." I didn't want him back in my ass until the second he said that. My balls must have shot a load of hormones into my brain at just that second. I was horny as hell and Vince's cock was the only thing that would hit the spot.

"I'm not a sex therapist," said Billy, "but let me suggest a change. You tops lie back and let Clydesdale and Mark sit on your cocks. Let them do the work for a while. That's the way I like it when I'm taking big meat. It's a good 'getting acquainted' position," That seemed like a good idea to me.

"Do you like big meat?" Mark asked. Billy was two inches shorter and 60 pounds heavier than me. His cock was half erect and had a filament of precum dripping from his slit. Mark reached over, intercepted a bead of precum and tasted it. "Not bad," he said with the air of a wine connoisseur tasting a new vintage. Everyone laughed.

"It sounds to me like you've been making a study of taking big cocks in small holes, Billy," Ram said. "Is it ready for publication yet?"

"There is still some field work to do," Billy said. I decided to try Billy's approach, so I straddled Vince and lowered my ass hole onto his cock. Billy had been watching and he re coated the monster with lube. It was still big, but since I was in control, it was much easier. I could stop and try again anytime I had a problem.

I had been half erect until he got five inches in, then I had a raging hard-on. Mark saw this and decided to followed suit. He knew a good thing when he saw it. Vince looked really happy as he cock went in deeper and deeper. Mark and I were face to face, so when Mark began his descent on Ram's cock I could see him.

It was nice to have someone take the ride with me. I knew he was feeling the same sensations as the cocks began to occupy our asses. Billy was right. I was a lot more comfortable with the monster in my ass. I even was doing the fancy dance on the love pole when it was fully embedded.

We broke apart again and regrouped. Mark and I sixty-nined while Vince fucked me speed eagle style and Ram took Mark doggy style. Ram popped first and that set off a chain reaction of orgasms. It turned out to be fun for everyone. Vince and Ram had a meeting early the next morning, so they had to leave. Billy left too.

Mark was usually always ready for a night cap, but he fell asleep. When I woke the next morning, it was nine already. I smelled bacon. Mark had made breakfast.

"It really takes it out of you, doesn't it?" Mark said. "I haven't slept past seven in years. Are you okay?"

"Sure. I have to admit feeling a bit stretched," I said. "You may not have noticed this, but I'm not a virgin, but I felt like a virgin last night."

"Me too, trusting myself to the kindness of gentlemen is a problem when the gentleman has the Dick of Death," Mark said. "It's strange. I felt naked. I was brought up a good southern Baptist and I felt that way in Junior High when I first showered with other guys. No kid was ever more embarrassed. I was already hairy and funny looking, thank God, my cock was big." he continued, then he paused.

"Did it bother you seeing the cock in my ass?" he asked. "I've never been fucked while another guy was sucking me. It kind of makes it difficult to have any secrets. Everything is either hard or oozing."

"It didn't bother me. Actually I think it turned me on," I said, "I looked up and saw your balls hanging there and then Ram's right next to them. I knew he was as deep as he could go. Ram moaned as he shot off and you began to shoot. It seemed his cock was forcing the cum from your balls. Every time he rammed you, you squirted."

"I just couldn't believe you could take it all," Mark said. "You are so small and it was so big. It seemed like a physical impossibility."

"Shit, it seemed that way to me a few times last night!" I said. The phone rang. It was John. One of the laborers on the job had found a five-gallon gas container. It was one of the containers that blew from the truck. It had a metal tag soldered to the underside of the tank. It said "Property of Victoriaville Farm and Seed." Victoriaville was eight miles from my hometown and the site of the Holy Roller Church Buddy's wife went to. A fucking clue at last, I thought.

I told John about my trip to the funeral and what I had suspected there.

"A fucking clue at last!" he said.

"You took the words out of my mouth! I think we need to have a meeting on this," I said. John told me everyone was out of town or busy. Sunday afternoon would be the first time we could get together. I said that I'd call Vince and let him in on it. John hung up.

I called Vince and woke him up. He said he'd get on it right away. Mark and I finished breakfast and went back to bed. We didn't sleep much. I was too excited and Mark was too horny. He seemed to think a good fucking would relax me. That made no sense to me at all, but it's what we did.

It turned out to be a good plan after all. After Vince, Mark was easy and he slid in and I went floating off to horny homosexual heaven. I couldn't believe how good it felt. Vince hadn't rearranged anything inside me and Mark's cock head felt like an old friend. We traded positions after a while and my cock seemed to fit his ass better and it seemed he enjoyed it more.

Over the next few hours we traded positions several times. I fucked him four times and he got me six. I have to admit I was getting to be partial to having Mark's meat probing my insides. It's hard to believe, but our adventure the night before with our horse hung friends must have opened us up. I was getting to be truly versatile. You can teach old dogs new tricks, if the tricks are fun. I knew things were changed when I fell asleep with Mark's cock in my ass. He fell asleep too. His cock was long enough to stay in, even when he was soft. I woke when he began to firm up again.

I twitched a few times and Mark did more than firm up. It was strange to have something growing in my ass. It was nice, but strange. The phone rang. It was Freddy Williams. He was downstairs and needed to talk. I broke off from Mark, showered and when down to the office.

Freddy and Billy were there. Freddy was our accountant-type partner. He had been running what we called the 'Nerd Patrol'. The 'Nerd Patrol' was cruising the Internet looking for clues. Most of the nerds were retired cops and firemen who had a lot of spare time. Several were on disability and the Patrol provided a welcome source of additional income.

They went hunting for web sites and chat rooms that were equivocal in their condemnation of the bombing. If you are on line for ten or twelve hours a day, you can do a lot of looking. There are thousands of sites, so you could only dent the potential. I thought it was a needle in the haystack. That isn't the way the Nerds saw it.

They entered each site into a common data base and Freddy compiled it. They searched it for repetitive entries. They also had separated anti-Semitic, anti-gay and anti-abortion sites. There was considerable overlap. The Anti-Gay-Anti-Abortion link was odd. The link between gays and abortion eluded me. I assumed that Jews were included as part of the great tradition of hate. They had summarized their searches the night before and Freddy wanted to go over the findings.

They too were beginning to focus on the Anti-Abortion angle. Virginia was a center for religious freaks. Richmond was surrounded by wackos in Tidewater and in the foothills of the Blue Ridge. Hate Christianity is a growth industry in Virginia. They pussyfooted around sponsorship of actual hate crimes. "Wink, wink, nod, nod," was their rule. Hatred is a much better tool for fund raising than love, peace and brotherhood. It's more fun to fight the devil than help the poor, or minister to the sick.

They needed enemies; our little section of Richmond's real estate was filled with enemies real and imagined. The preachers pretended they wanted them to be vanquished by lightening strikes, fire and brimstone, but they would settle for explosives in a pinch.

Freddy had done a thorough job. Computer types aren't prone to be sloppy and the Nerd Patrol was no exception. They had found 5,320 sites and had 370 major ones. Many of the lesser sites were take-offs of the bigger ones, with no new materials. They copied or plagiarized the big boys. I asked how many were in Virginia. Most didn't indicate where they were, but 271 identified Virginia as their home.

Several of the Nerds had joined in hate chat rooms and became regulars. They posed as potential converts. Freddy was deep into three or four local chat rooms and had a good feel for what was going on.

"The phrase which pops up is "doing God's work" I've been finding that in several Bible Thumper rooms," Freddy said. "Carl and Lou have been encountering it elsewhere in Virginia. The Tidewater groups seem to be comparatively quiet, but the Piedmont areas are awash in it."

"Do you think it's an accidental recurrence?" Billy asked.

"I thought it might be, but Carl thinks it's an official line. Someone has been proposing it as a justification for the bombing," Freddy said. "Carl's really into chat rooms and knows their dynamics. He says you usually don't find repetitive comments, unless it appears in the mass media or on what I call the fruit and nut call in programs. Carl listens to them too."

"Who is Carl?" I asked.

"He's a 74 year old, retired fireman," Freddy answered. "I think he was way to the right, until this happened. Killing firemen was too much for him."

"No chance he's giving information to the other side, is there?"

"His Grandson was the fireman, burned alive in his truck next to the temple," Freddy said.

"I'm sorry," I said. "I didn't know."

"You're right to ask, we don't need spies," Freddy replied. "Carl's bedridden now, he's got diabetes bad, so couldn't get to the funeral. He doesn't sleep, he just searches the net, looking for clues."

"Does he have a theory?" I asked.

"He seems to be focusing on a group in South-West Virginia between Lynchburg and the North Carolina border..," Freddy said.

"That's my stomping grounds," I exclaimed. "Damn! I was there last week."

"Did you notice any strange religious groups springing up there?"

"As a matter of fact I did," I said with the flair of a magician. "There is an odd group there and I have the local cops looking into it already." I explained my cousin Buddy's situation and the group his wife had taken up with.

I was on the phone to Buddy and got the particulars. The Church was called the Victory Temple and the preacher was Dr. Lucas Paul. It was the sole remaining building in what had been Victoriaville, Virginia. It had been the Victoriaville Methodist Church and they were able to reuse part of the sign. "Cheep-ass Bastards" was the way Buddy described them. I told him to keep this call close to his chest. He said, the sheriff was coming over that night and he would have him call me.

Freddy called Carl and told him the names. He said Carl would look into it immediately.

Mark came down from my apartment and said, hello. Freddy hadn't met him before. Billy had been there the night before. I had a feeling Billy had let Freddy know the details of last nights festivities.

Freddy had an odd approach to sex. He looked like a middle-aged accountant who would only have sex with his laptop. He was a horny guy and seemed to be genuinely bisexual. He had a girl friend he had met at a swinger's group. He also liked men. He didn't mix the two interests. The woman didn't know of his interest in men. I could sense Freddy was ready for some relaxation time. I was a good two hours since the last time I shoot off. It seemed to me some relaxation was in order.

Part 6

After Mark and my experiments with bottoming, Billy and Freddy were a nice return to our normal patterns. Billy tended to like the bottom anyway and he had been watching more than doing the night before. He was a short, stocky guy with a tight ass. It took a while, but I got in and he got off.

I will say he was a sensible and appreciative bottom. He knew my cock was near the upper limit of his ass's ability to stretch. He was willing and knew it might not be easy. I don't like fucking guys who are whiners. After my time with Vince I knew what he was feeling as I worked my cock in the hole. I took it slow and easy and I hit pay dirt on my third try.

Billy was sitting back on my love pole when he began to quiver. He turned into a rag doll on a stick as he relaxed. My cock must have been close to touching his heart, it went so deep. I wasn't sure there was room for my cock and his prostate, it was so tight. I think I squeezed his prostate really hard. When he popped, I could feel his ass contracting well before the cum sprayed me.

I've felt prostates just before the orgasm. They fill and turn rock hard. I think my cock kept the prostate from filling easily, Billy's orgasm was in slow motion. He had been twitching for almost a minute before any of the white stuff spurted from his piss slit.

He was a wet dishrag after he popped. I rolled him over and screwed him doggy style for a while. He wasn't too enthusiastic about that at first. He had just shot and had lost interest. Much to my surprise, I found the groove, the spot in an ass when the cock and chute are perfectly matched. He was moaning after a few thrusts and damn if he didn't shoot again.

I guess Freddy and Mark were doing something. By the time I paid any attention, they were both sleeping. I know a good idea when I see it, so I took a nap. Billy woke me easing his cock into my ass. His cock is nice and thin, so it was pleasant stimulation without the drama of Vince's meat. Mark and Freddy got up, saw Billy humping me and asked if they could join in. Where there's a will there's a way.

Somehow the anatomy was right and we had a nice four man fuck. I was in Billy while Freddy was in me with Mark poking Fred.

Late Tuesday, Sheriff Earl Evans called me. He was tracing the gasoline containers and was hot on the trail of the Born Agains. He also thought it might be good time for me to drop by and check things out in person. Apparently, we were the only ones following the trail. Neither the Richmond Police, nor the State Troopers had been by to see Earl. I remembered my momma had a birthday on Thursday, so if I visited I would get points for being a good son, as well as check out the scene in Victoriaville.

I drove home on Wednesday, taking a detour through Victoriaville. Victoriaville was a crossroads, with a church and an abandoned gas station and a thicket which had grown around the ruins of the feed store. The wooden buildings had all fallen down, the concrete block buildings were walls only, with collapsed roofs. There were several farms nearby, but most were no longer actively farmed and scrub growth was replacing the fields.

Victoriaville had been a small community at its height, but it was only a few houses when I was a kid. The railroad siding that justified the community had been discontinued in the early '50s. The church alone remained in use. It was a large wooden building, now covered in brick-like asphalt shingles. There were several trailers to the rear. One was labeled 'Office", the other

'Youth Center'. There were several beaten up pick-ups in the parking area, one Dodge Dart that had seen better days and a shiny new Lincoln Town Car.

I assumed the Reverend owned the Town Car. I had a good many preconceptions about the man, and the Town Car confirmed most of them.

Cousin Buddy's farm was about six miles down the road, so I dropped in to see how he was doing. He was on a tractor mowing a field of hay. He couldn't hear me drive up over the noise of the tractor, so I watched him work for a while before he saw me. When he did, he drove over. We went to the house and he gave me a beer. This was a shock, he never had a beer in the house before. He had been a classic Baptist drinker, behind the barn, or at a hunting club.

"How goes things with your wife?" I asked.

"Not good," he said. Buddy was real nervous, glad to see me but uncomfortable. "She doesn't let me see the kids anymore. I'm a bad influence."

"Have you been to court?"

"Sure. I've got visitation, but she says it's God's Law," Buddy said with disgust in his voice. "Ronnie sneaks out to see me, but the others are too young." Ronnie was his oldest kid, eleven I think. "Your Momma brings them over when she can."

"Its' rough," I said. "It will work out somehow."

"Clydesdale. Do you think I'm a bad father?" Buddy asked. "I seem to be turning gay. I never did anything like that the other day with Earl before."

"You didn't like it?" I asked.

"That's the problem. I liked it a lot."

"Then what's the problem?"

"You've always been a cock hound, Clydesdale." Buddy said. "I never fucked anyone, except my wife. I kept myself pure for her. She's left me and I slip my dick into Earl's ass and I love it."

"Shit Buddy! You didn't get Earl pregnant did you?" I asked. Buddy burst out laughing. "You know he wasn't a virgin. You saw me poke him and open him up for you," I said. "He liked it, you liked it, we're all adults, what's the problem?"

"I never minded playing with you boys, but Earl is different. I don't think I'm ready to be gay," Buddy said. "If Sally finds out, I'm dead meat."

"Buddy, you can't make yourself like, what you don't like. You can pretend, but believe me it won't work. I tried it," I said. "You and Earl are friends and unless I'm real mistaken, you both like sex together. Earl's not going to marry you and put your picture on the social page of the paper as his wife. You'd look like shit in a white dress and veil. You're friends, you might as well enjoy it."

"It isn't just Earl," Buddy said. A car drove up. It was Buck Williams. He had been one of our childhood playmates. We also had messed around some when we were teenagers. I realized Buddy was nervous because I had walked in on a date. I looked at Buddy and he had a sheepish look on his face.

At fifteen Buck was a skinny kid, a basketball star. At 45 he was strapping. He had filled out, and looked muscular now. The truck said, Williams & Daughter, Construction. He had the brown, tanned look of a man who spent most of his life outside. His brown hair and close cropped beard were almost the color of his skin. Buck waved and got out of the car.

"Clydesdale! Good to see you," Buck said. "Has it been 30 years?"

"I must be. You're looking good," I said.

"You're looking the same," he said, then he laughed. He had been the class dream boat, I was the class freak. "I saw you in the papers. That was an awful thing that happened." We talked about the bombing.

"Your daughter is working with you?" I said. "That's unusual in construction."

"It's not 100% on purpose. She went to college, came home and married her High School sweetheart and farm boy. They had two kids and he goes and gets religion. He gets it bad and left her to follow the master. I get my daughter back and the grand kids."

"You don't look old enough to be a granddaddy," I said.

"When you start at 17, you get a lot of living done young," Buck said. "Ellen's a good girl and she has been great for the business. Did you know that Sue Ellen died four years ago? Cancer."

"No I didn't. Momma must be losing her touch," I said. "I'm real sorry, she was a pretty woman. Did your daughter's hubby find God in the same place as Buddy's wife did?"

"Damn right. And I don't think God had anything to do with it," Buck said. "Ovid was a nice boy, had been in the army and done well. He just was born to follow. He has no fucking common sense either."

"What did he do in the army?" I asked. Where that question came from, I don't know. It seemed to shoot into my head from outer space.

"Ordinance, demolition, that sort of stuff," Buck said. "He was a big shot there. Something went wrong. He was going to be a career man, but left. The army may say it trains you for civilian life, but nothing he learned was helpful for running a dairy farm." He paused. "Are you still a cock hound? I always figured you left town because you had screwed every willing ass here and wanted to find more men."

"I sure am. Getting better at it too," I said.

"You know, fifteen years ago, I felt real superior to you," Buck said. "I thought I had it all figured out. Everything was going my way."

"And now?" I asked.

"I feel nothing, but pure unadulterated envy!" Buck said. "Things aren't black and white, hetro or homo. It's all confused. I've been screwed over by the God fearing fakers and helped by my closet case friends."

"I always guessed you had a small warm spot for cock," I said. I had picked him up late one night after a big game, when he had a few too many beers and had run his car into a ditch. I got it out, him home, and sucked him to boot. He pretended it was the beer.

"I have more than a small warm spot, as it turns out," Buck continued. "I came close to doing something real stupid after Sue Ellen died. Earl got me in time, took he home and got me straight."

"Did he get you in bed too?" I asked.

"That he did!" Buck admitted. "I was lonely and a bit drunk and was in bed and one thing led to another. Damn if I didn't have the best sex I ever had. I didn't know it could be that good. Sue Ellen was nice, but never really enjoyed it. Earl did. I realized I liked it and had missed out on a lot."

"I've missed damn little!" I said. I didn't want to horn in on their fun. "I've got to be heading off to see Mom."

"Are you staying with her?" Buck asked.

"Nope. I'm bunking at the Colonial Motel. All my Aunts have arrived for the birthday. They've filled up the house." We said goodbye and I went into town to see Mom. I was wondering what chance there was that Buck would drop in to see me sometime during my stay. My guess was it was more than a fifty-fifty chance.

Mom's house was filled with my three aunts. Aunts Ellen and Becky were fine. Aunt Edith was as sour a woman who ever lived. When I was little, I thought she just plain hated me and wanted to make my life as miserable as possible. When I was a teenager I thought she guessed I was gay and hated me because of that. Momma told me Edith treated everyone like trash and scum. She had never been nice to anyone in her life. The world just wasn't good enough for her, she deserved a better place.

I talked for a while, then went to the motel to check in. I wandered by the Police Station and saw Earl on the street getting in his cruiser. He told me we needed to talk, privately. I said, I was at the motel in room 104 and would be back at my room by nine. He told me he was busy and asked if I was an early riser. I said, I got up around 5:30 and he suggested we could have breakfast together. He wasn't due at work until 8:30. I went back to Mom's.

Mom tended to give into Aunt Edith. She hated a scene, but Becky and Ellen never considered that possibility. They would do battle with her at every opportunity. My picture leading the kids to safety carrying the Torah caused quite a stir. It had hit the national media and Becky had laminated the newspaper picture in plastic, so she could show her friends.

"Were there any Christian children in that part of town?" Edith asked. She clearly seemed to think I had saved unworthy children. I wanted to say something nasty, but Ellen beat me to the punch.

"What are you thinking? Have you gone crazy, Edith? I heard you say some awful things, but that takes the cake!" Ellen exploded.

"You call yourself a Christian, but I don't see any Christian love, or charity or..." Becky said, sputtering as she tried to find words. "You should be ashamed!" Edith tried a counterattack.

"That whole city is filled with Gays and abortionists and Jew...," Edith realized she was treading on thin ice and pulled back. "Just the same, there is a lot of sin in the city!"

"There sure is and there's none here. Remember Cousin Lonnie? Reverend Dennis?" Ellen asked. Lonnie set fires and Dennis raped a fifteen year old girl. Ellen was merciful. Edith's husband was town florist and gay as a goose. He was a nice man with a heart of gold and loved by everyone, but as macho as the orchids he grew. They never had children and my Aunts felt he wasn't capable of intercourse. No one ever mentioned that.

"If I recall, Dennis was your favorite preacher. You were on the selection committee," Ellen said. "You like that charlatan preacher at Victoriaville. Given your track record, I'd keep my eye on that fool."

"Dr. Paul is a true Christian!" Edith retorted. "Doing battle against sin and the devil! Trying to save all those unborn children."

"Edith! What in hell are you worried about unborn children for?" Becky cried. Aunt Becky never said words like hell, so she must have been mighty exercised. "You have four nephews and six nieces and you never said a pleasant word to them. You want more children in the world, so you can be nasty to them?"

"Clydesdale saves a hundred kids from being blown to bits and you complain, then you talk about unborn children! What are you thinking, Edith?" Ellen asked. "You worry about the unborn and salvation after death. Why don't you worry about the living?" Usually this sort of fight occurred on the third or forth day of a visit. To have it on the first day was a record of sorts. The doorbell rang and two of Mom's friends appeared bearing gifts. None of my Aunts ever fought in public, so everything calmed down. The rest of the afternoon was pleasantly spent in reminiscing.

We went out to dinner that night to Elmer's Steak House. It had been the only restaurant in town when I was a kid and had a loyal, but elderly clientèle. Elmer was dead, but Young Elmer was running the place. They had actually changed the menu and the food was simple, but better than I remembered.

I dropped off my Aunts at home after dinner and went to my room at the Colonial. The motel was the same age as Elmer's, but had been renovated recently and the room looked new. I called and left a message at the office saying I had a possible explosive expert associated with the Victory Temple. I had just finished when, there was a knock at the door. It was Buck.

"Come on in. I was expecting you," I said, opening the door.

"Is it that obvious?" Buck asked looking embarrassed.

"Not really. I just asked myself what I would do if I were in your situation. I figured I drop by and renew old acquaintances."

"Like to talk?" he said.

"Sure, but I'm horny as hell. Let's get naked and talk," I suggested. That was fine with him and I was surprised how fast he stripped and went after my cock. Buck may have been new to the gay scene, but he knew his way around a cock.

We got on the bed when he came up for air.

"I've been thinking about your cock for thirty years." he said.

"I thought you were drunk and didn't know what you were doing?"

"You didn't believe that, did you?"

"Not for a minute," I said. "I don't mind a guy pretending, if I get some cock."

"The jokes on me," Buck said. "It turns out I'm a size queen. I was afraid to suck it then, but it's been in my dreams ever since."

"You dream about me?"

"No. I dream about your cock!" he said laughing. I pivoted on the bed and began sucking him as he returned to my cock. Buck was a handsome man and he got better looking as he aged. He had a nice cock. I deep throated him and much to my surprise, he did the same to me. Not many guys can do that. I was getting real close, so I asked him if he wanted to take my load.

"I don't usually. I only eat my own," he said. "Tell me when you are ready and I will make up my mind then."

"Fair enough." I replied. I know some guys who like to shoot without warning, but I think if a guy is nice enough to suck your cock, you should be polite. Cock sucking is so in your face anyway, there is no need to drain you balls in a guys mouth if he doesn't want it. A minute or two later I told him I was on the edge.

Buck pulled off, then deep throated me again. My cock almost exploded. It was great. A few seconds later my mouth was filled with his seed. We ate each other's cum and then lay there, licking up what ever dripped and oozed from our cocks. I pivoted again. Buck looked at me. I opened my mouth. I hadn't swallowed, so he saw his cock cream. He kissed me and ate his own sperm.

"I don't need to go home tonight," he said.

"That's fine with me. The Sheriff will be coming by tomorrow morning."

"I know. He said he would be by," Buck said. "He thought you wouldn't mind a threesome."

"He was absolutely right about that," I said.

Part 7

I woke at 5:30 hearing Buck's moans. The Sheriff had his cock deep in Buck's ass. Earl saw me open my eyes.

"I tried to wait until a more decent hour, but I just couldn't hold back," Earl said. "I figured I'd do some in depth investigation."

"That's fine with me. I'm not opposed to some investigation myself," I said.

"Do you mind if I take a breather and let Clydesdale take me for a spin around the block?" Earl asked Buck.

"You will come back and finish me off?" Buck asked.

"Either I'll do it or Clydesdale will. We're all friends, aren't we?"

"He's awfully big." Buck said, sounding a bit uncertain. My cock had met his tonsils, but the night's play had been all oral. I love to fuck, but I had fallen asleep before I had a chance to bring the subject up.

"We can play it by ear. There is this powerful itch in my ass that Clydesdale needs to scratch!" Earl said. Earl pulled out of Buck, got on his back on the edge of the bed and put his feet on my shoulders. I shoved in to the hilt on the first thrust. That isn't usually the nicest way to do that, but I had a suspicion Earl would like it. I was right. The precum stated to flow from his cock like a mountain stream in flood. He was one happy man.

"I forgot to tell you," I said. "I ain't rushed one little bit this morning. You are on a local, not an express. I want to take my time." Earl smiled. Buck straddled Earl's head and let the sheriff suck his balls. I had a feeling he wanted him to eat his ass, but was shy.

"Shit it's big." Buck said looking at my donkey dong. I pulled out, so only the tip of the head was in Earl's ass. I slowly slipped it in, so Buck could see every inch disappear. I pulled it out again.

"Tempted?" I asked. We were facing each other across Earl's body. Buck's cock was hard and pointing up to the ceiling. "Is it watching my cock or feeling Earl's tongue in your ass that's turning you on?"

"That's a really hard question. I don't really know," Buck said. "Do you think it will fit?"

"It's hard to tell until you try it," I replied. "I've been in one or two asses in my day and you never know. Sucking is pretty dependable. You find a bad sucker once in a while, but that's rare. Fucking is a crap shoot. It depends on the cock and the ass. Sometimes it doesn't work at all. The cock's too big, or the ass is too small. Sometimes it just doesn't do nothing. It's as if your cock misses every good spot. But when it is good, it's great. Like it is for Earl now."

Earl moaned in agreement. "I love to top and never much liked the bottom. My cock feels great in a quivering ass. My ass is worth shit," I continued.

"You never liked it in the ass?" Buck asked.

"Never until a month ago," I said. "I ended up getting poked by a goofy looking EMT. Mark doesn't look like much, but his cock and my ass were made for each other. I couldn't believe it. It was good." I was getting close, so

I slicked some lube on Earl's cock and pulled out of his ass. Then I straddled him and sat back on his throbbing cock.

Earl's cock wasn't a perfect fit for my ass, but it was damn good. Buck took some initiative of his own and got Earl's legs in the air again and he popped his cock in the Sheriff's hole. Earl looked as if he were going to pass out.

Buck had been the football team Captain in school and team work was his specialty. Within a few seconds Buck had me lifting up on Earl's cock and then sitting back as he pulled out and rammed in. We tried a variant, I would be up when Buck thrust in. It was hard to believe you could have so much cock and ass in one area. Earl was shivering so bad I could hardly hold him down.

If I were a betting man, I would bet Earl had the best orgasm in his life that morning. I couldn't believe how long that puppy twitched. We disentangled ourselves. Buck looked at me and I looked at him. He bent over and opened wide. He winced a few times as I slowly worked my way into his love tunnel.

He lost his erection and I was about to give up, when I hit a good spot. It was the right spot, maybe not as good as the place deep in Earl's ass, but really good. When he began to enjoy it, my cock responded accordingly and that extra bit of size really hit the bull's eye for Buck. I flopped him over from doggy style to spread eagle and he liked that a lot too. All in all, it was good morning sexually.

"Damn. I'm getting close. I want it to last and can't do it pumping you," I told Buck. Buck looked uncertain.

"I really wouldn't mind giving you a ride," he said, "Do you think that would be okay?" I'm a sucker for a guy who asks politely. I traded places with Buck. He slowly slipped his six incher into my cum lubricated ass. It was just the right size for a social fuck.

"What does this Preacher man, Dr. Paul, have that attracts people?" I asked.

"Simple answers for complex questions. Everything is black and white," Buck said. "My daughter says it's all black and white, no grays, and most of all, no color. She says they think you are either 100% virtuous and Christian, or you deserve the death penalty." Earl rallied and joined in the conversation.

"The guy reminds me of John Brown," Earl added. "I am a true son of Virginia, I was brought up to hate him, but slavery was bad and needed to be done away with. John Brown was right about that. It was everything else he was wrong about. Mass murder and insurrection can't be the first step to achieving paradise."

"My daughter didn't agree with Ovid, her husband, and he tried to beat her," Buck said. "She was a 'disobedient daughter of Eve,' he said. She took off with the kids and moved in with me. Ovid even tried to change his name to Matthew, because Ovid was a pagan poet! The preacher seemed to think regular beatings were the way to find God. I hate to sound like a pop psychiatrist, but Dr. Paul liked beatings and absolute obedience a bit more than is healthy. He wants his flock to prove how much they love whatever he thinks of as God." Buck was slow fucking and doing a good job of it. I was enjoying myself more than I expected.

"Some people like that stuff. He told them you can't live with an infidel. That's what screwed up Buddy's wife. Buddy's sweet, loving, kind, considerate and a good provider, but that doesn't count," Earl said. "You need to demonstrate in front of women's clinics, you need to attack gays, lesbians and radical feminists, if you are to be saved. All sins are equal. Having a beer after work is just as bad as killing someone. Sin is sin and you'll go to hell, if you don't do exactly what the preacher says."

I told Buck I was getting stiff, so we traded places. Buck was nice and relaxed now. I slipped in with no problem. I went in slow and watched him. When my cock head hit the right spot, Buck moaned. I pulled back and tried it again. Buck had the same reaction and I rubbed my cock head over the spot a few times in quick succession.

"Clydesdale, watching you fuck must be like having watched Michelangelo painting the Sistine Chapel. You're a master at it," Earl said. Buck didn't say anything because he was shooting his load all over his chest. It was a hands free orgasm. As I said, Buck was a handsome man and he knew it. He usually had every hair in place. The sperm sprayed over his gut and chest and was messy, but kind of pretty. It was good to see him so relaxed and unconcerned.

"You haven't popped yet, have you?" Earl asked.

"Nope," I said, "but you need more recovery time, don't you"

"Yes, but I am nothing if not a good sport," the Sheriff answered. "I'm willing."

"I like it better if my partner is really enthusiastic," I said. "What chance is there that I may be able to work some play time in later today?" Earl smiled.

"I would guess you've got a real good chance," he said. That was good enough for me. Buck had to leave, so he showered and went to work. Earl and I spent the next hour talking about the Victory Temple. Earl had the Southern Sheriff look down solid, but he was no slouch in the investigative

department. It helped that nothing ever happened in town, so people tended to remember things.

The auction of the Victoriaville Seed and Feed had been a big event fifteen years before. It had gone out of business just after a delivery of six new tractors. They were available at a real good price. The gasoline containers were made with name tags after several people failed to return the older, unlabeled containers, pissing the owner off. He had name plates welded to fifty brand new containers. This had been a year before the auction and the sheriff assumed all were sold.

"The auctioneer remembered them. He sold them in lots of ten and this caused a stir. Several guys wanted them sold individually, because they only wanted one," Earl said. "The volunteer fire department bought 20, as did the ESSO station. Ten went to Clem Jones, the dairy farmer." Something clicked in my head. I almost remembered something, but it wouldn't come into focus.

"I'm tracing down the remaining containers. I have a deputy looking into them now," Earl said. "I have two contacts inside the church. Damn if it doesn't bother me to call that place a church!" The phone rang. It was Mom who needed me home. The party was that afternoon and some furniture needed to be moved. I said I would come.

Earl and I showered and went our ways. Earl said, he had some meetings at the Court House and would get back to me later. I got another call. It was my Aunt Becky. She apologized for calling, but she wanted me to get a haircut and mustache trim. Becky said she knew it was stupid, but Mom didn't like my handlebar, sideburns and beard. It would mean a lot to her if the pictures of the party were of me trimmed and neat. I said sure.

I dropped in at the local barber shop and was shorn. This nice woman took her time and when I looked in the mirror after she was done, I hardly recognized myself. I sported a handlebar mustache and a two pronged goatee. I had sideburns and hadn't shaved in a week. When she was finished I looked like a banker, or a college professor. I had a carefully groomed beard and trimmed mustache. I didn't look like a redneck at all.

The woman looked at me. "I should have taken a picture of you before! No one would believe it," she said, then she quickly apologized. "It's not that you weren't... interesting before." I stopped her and said I knew exactly what she meant. It was hard to believe. It only cost me twelve dollars. I couldn't believe that either.

Mom almost cried when she saw me. The new look was a hit. Edith refused to believe it was me, until I talked. We had a good day. I moved the furniture and talked with my Aunts and Mom and caught up on all the relatives. The party was nice. Everyone I knew growing up was a lot older, but I was closer to being famous than any of them were. I had my picture in the nation wide media and Mom loved every minute.

I hadn't exactly been a trial when I was growing up, but I wasn't everyone's idea of a dream child either. Mom had always defended me and now her faith in me was justified to all. Mom didn't crow. She left that to Aunts Ellen and Becky. A few cousins came, it was a midweek party and most had to work.

I was hoping to find out more about the Victory Temple, but Mom moved in solidly Methodist and Presbyterian circles and they didn't associate with Victory Temple types. The only luck I had was with the Presbyterian Minister, Rev. William Williams. He was a young guy, outgoing and about as unlike the Ministers I remembered as a kid as he could be. I was telling my story about the explosion and walking through the broken stained glass windows. The glass was almost like snow on the ground, but brightly colored.

He wanted to know what was being done about them. I told him what I knew. He said, he wanted to organize a campaign to raise money to replace them. He figured if several hundred churches contributed some money, they could replace the windows. He had mentioned it to some of the local Ministers, and they were interested. It seemed like a good idea to me.

I asked, if the Victory Temple would contribute. A cloud came over his face. "As far as I can tell, the only charity that place supports is the Dr. Paul Retirement Fund," Williams said. "I try to be charitable, but it's hard. He writes these awful letters to the papers. I write rebuttals and my wife gets death threats."

"Death threats?" I asked.

"Well, more prank calls than death threats," Williams said. A woman walked up beside him.

"Will, tell the truth! They are genuine, 100% real, death threats," she said. He introduced the woman as his wife, Julia.

"Have you told the police about these threats?" I asked.

"No, I really think they are prank calls," Rev. Williams said again. Julia disagreed and I had to think that she might well be right. "I do despise that group. Harmless threats are one thing. Tearing families apart is quite another. Two years ago, Elder Clem Jones died and his grandson didn't even come to the funeral. Ovid said, he wouldn't go into a house of sin."

"How in hell can a Presbyterian Church be a house of sin!" Julia asked. It was becoming clear that Julia Williams was my kind of woman. "The poor man left Ovid everything he owned. Ovid turned into a pompous and sanctimonious prick!" She looked at me and blushed. "I am sorry, I think I just flunked another test in the meek and mild Presbyterian Minister's wife curriculum." My Aunt Ellen was walking by and said, "And we love you for it dear!" I laughed.

"It sounds to me like you are on the mark," I said, "My cousin, Buddy, has the same problems."

"You are Buddy and Sally's cousin?" Williams asked. "He's a good man. I'm really worried about the children who fall into the cults grasp. They carry the 'Spare the rod and spoil the child' maxim to an extreme. I've been trying to get county welfare to look into it, but they won't touch it with a ten-foot pole. I'm on the School Board and we need to try to save them."

My Mom came by to make sure I saw Mr. Edland, my high school history teacher. I had no idea he was still alive. He looked exactly the same, only more so. He told me, I looked like King George V. I asked, if that was good and he said, it was a damn sight better than any other look I had tried. He asked about the bombing. Mr. Edland had been in Europe with Eisenhower. He had told us stories about the Blitz of London and fighting the Nazis.

"It looks to me like we may have the same types after us again," he said. "Do you think these are home grown?"

"I'm afraid I do," I said.

"I wish I could fight again," he said. "You'll have to fight for me."

"I already am," I said. Mr. Edland shook my hand.

Aunt Becky came by and asked me to move Rev. Williams' car, so Aunt Edith could leave. She gave me the keys and told me it was a black Taurus. There were two almost identical cars in the driveway. I tried the keys in one and they didn't work, so I opened the other. I should have known that Edith would drive something odd and unattractive,. She must have been the only person in Virginia to drive a Pacer. Edith left early, I assumed there was too much good will in the house for her to be happy.

The party wound down and I helped clean up. Momma and the remaining Aunts were tired, so I went back to the Motel. Mom packed me a care package of left over food, just in case I got hungry on the drive to the Motel. Sometimes Mothers can't stop being Mothers.

I got a call from Earl at 7:00. He was at an accident and would come by after it was cleared up. He arrived at 8:30 with Buddy and a deputy named Slim. They all devoured the care package and we settled down to a nice evening of sex.

Part 8

Earl told me I would like Slim. He was right. Slim Wilson, the Deputy, was a trip. I thought I was country. Slim defined country. He was from some God forsaken place in the mountains. He was tall, slim, redheaded with a close cropped mustache and goatee. I knew the close cropping was a requirement of the job. Deep in his heart he would like to look like a Billy-Goat.

I also thought I liked sex. Slim ate it up. His cock, mouth and ass were everywhere. He wasn't shy about anything. Shoving a cock in an ass was no more to him than shaking hands. He really hit it off with Buddy.

Buddy was basically an up tight Southern Baptist boy. As far as I could tell, Slim was a real laid back Druid. I think Buddy was shocked when he first played with Slim. His approach to sex was so casual and unashamed. Buddy thought he was odd. That all changed when he fucked Slim the first time. Buddy's cock was made for Slim's ass. I could see Buddy glowing as he slipped into the shit chute. He enjoyed it so much, he was embarrassed. I knew Buddy liked Earl. I think Buddy got so carried away and he was afraid Earl would be jealous.

Earl came over to Slim and fed him his cock. Slim licked the Sheriff's cock and balls. Earl kissed Buddy as Buddy continued to pump. Slim liked being rear ended as he was front loaded. It was hot to watch, but it was better for them than it was for me. Buddy discovered that good sex and love weren't the same thing. Earl didn't mind if he played with other men. Earl knew Buddy was his.

Slim had nice equipment, not challenging, but fun. His cock was okay, but Slim's ass hole was his best sex organ. When Buddy popped and pulled out, I moved in. I admit Buddy's cum made a good lubricant, but Slim was a first rate bottom. He liked it and you could tell. He seemed to be able to constrict his ass to grab my cock and massage it. After my recent experiences with bottoming I knew it was hard to do when you're stretched to the limit.

I don't have the biggest cock in the world, but I am in what they called in school the "ninetieth percentile". Slim took it well and willingly. He had a great time and gave as good as he got. I shot off and took a breather. I must have slept for a while. When I woke, Earl was next to me. He was awake too, so I started sucking him. Slim slipped his dick in my ass. It was a nice touch.

Earl rotated so we could 69. Buddy rear ended him as Slim continued to fuck me. We had all shot off earlier, so it was a nice quiet time. It was more of a cock massaging my prostate than a real fucking. I could watch Buddy slow pumping Earl's ass and taste Earl's cock juice as it dribbled. Earl was tasting my juice, as Slim slowly thrust in my hole.

I don't know how long we did it. It was a long while. I was thinking, we could do it all night long, when Buddy began to pick up steam. Cocks are tricky things. They seem to have a mind of their own. I could sense Buddy's balls filling and soon we all got back into the mood. Earl shot first and set off a chain reaction. I shot a huge load into Earl's mouth and fell asleep.

I woke at five and Earl's cock was six inches from my mouth. I decided to find out what dried cum tastes like, so I sucked him. It was nice to suck a man from being completely soft to being hard. Earl told me he liked being sucked awake. Better than an alarm clock, he said. He wanted to get into work early and check on Mr. Edland. I asked, what was wrong with Mr. Edland. Earl told me, Edland had been in the accident that delayed him.

Buddy had to tend to his cows and left Slim and me to our own devices. He said, he would really like to spend some time getting to know my prostate. I told him that would be fine, if he would teach me what he did with his ass when he was fucked.

He was a good teacher. Maybe he was too good. He shot off ten minutes into his lesson. He told me, we could finish it some other time. The phone rang. It was Earl. Edland was in critical condition. The mechanic who examined the car said, the brakes had been tampered with, almost cut through. It all became clear to me.

"It was Williams they were after," I said.

"What are you talking about?" Earl asked.

"Rev. Williams. He's been getting death threats from the Victory Temple people," I said. "Edland parked next to him at the party at Mom's house. They have almost identical cars."

"Shit!" Earl exclaimed. "Williams never told me about the threats."

"He thought they were pranksters. His wife thought they were real," I said. "She's a smart woman."

"Holy Shit! I can't believe people hide things like that. Threats are a crime too! Is Slim still there?" I said, yes. "Send him over, if you will. We've got some detecting to do!" Earl hung up.

I told Slim what happened. He was the 'fingerprint man' for the town and was on his way to the Police Station in thirty seconds flat. I got dressed and went to Mom's house for breakfast.

The local jungle drums were working at full speed. Old ladies have a remarkable communication system. Mom and my Aunts knew all about the accident, Mr. Edland's status in the hospital and they had a suspicion something was wrong.

"Edward was such a careful man. He had that car checked every six months and was so particular. I can't believe the brakes failed," Mom said.

"Maybe he was getting sloppy in his old age?" Edith said.

"I just don't know why you say things like that," Aunt Becky said. "You know what he is like. Precise and exact. He's no different now than when he taught my daughter 35 years ago." That started an argument, so I went to help Mom and Aunt Ellen in the kitchen.

"Clydesdale, did you notice how similar Rev. Williams' car was to Mr. Edland's?" Mom asked.

"I sure did Mom."

"Do you think someone should mention that to the Sheriff?" Mom continued. "It's very worrisome. They should have reported their problem to the Police."

"I already have Momma. It might be nice if you kept it quiet like. It would be better if nobody knew for a while."

"Edith is in deep with those people. She has less sense now than when she was a girl," Ellen said. "She might report back anything she hears. We need a little trip. Let's get her out of town for a few days." Ellen was super organized and she called a travel agent friend and had reservations at the Peaks of Otter Lodge in a few minutes. I remembered the Blue Ridge was Edith's favorite vacation spot.

Ellen presented it as a special birthday gift to Mom from her children. Edith said there was too much to clean up at the house after the party. Ellen told them I had volunteered to do that while they were gone. I would stay in the house.

"If we leave now, we can be there in time for lunch!" Becky said. "They have fresh caught Mountain Bass this time of the year," Forty five minutes later, they were on their way in Becky's Oldsmobile. Ellen was prone to impulsive gestures like the trip to the mountains and all four women were enthusiastic. They had done that sort of thing when they were girls and were acting like young girls as they drove off.

I called Earl and told him about Mom's suspicions. Mom wasn't exactly Sherlock Holmes. If she could figure it out, others would. He wanted to keep as quiet as possible and asked me to look at the driveway and see if there was anything of interest there.

He hung up and I called the office to see what was up in Richmond. Butch was at the phone and I gave him a full report. He would look up Ovid Jones and see if he was on any watch list. Butch told me an Internet server named "eog.com" seemed to be the locale for several of the most radical web sites. It was located somewhere in the area. He asked me to stay near the phone so he could get back to me.

I went to the yard and gave it a quick look. It didn't need any more than that. There was the stain of break fluid, where Edland's car had been. I got a camera and took pictures. I called Earl and got Slim. He said, he'd be by to take evidence. I went to the motel and checked out then relocated to the attic of Mom's house.

I cleaned up the party stuff and decided to trim the shrubs. Mom had a cell phone, so I could keep in touch while outside. I wanted to be in the yard to see if any of the neighbors might have seen something. It was a weekday and the street was quiet. The shrubs needed a lot of work and I got into it and had a good time. It was a hot day and it was nice to have some real physical work to do.

Several neighbors walked by, but hadn't seen anything. A woman came by and wanted to root cuttings for the shrub I was trimming. By lunch time, I was bushed and went in for a lunch of leftover party food. The day had turned really hot. After lunch, I went out to survey my work. The house looked like the Titanic going down for the last time. I had trimmed half and that part looked great. The other half was shaggy and disreputable. It was twice as tall and the house looked like it had a list. I would have to do the rest.

After ten minutes, I was sweating like a pig and took off my shirt. Several people honked their horns in greeting, but it was so hot, few were out walking. There were a few kids on bicycles going off to the pool. One kid came by several times. I would guess he was a senior in high school. On his third trip by the house, he was going slower and looking me over good. I knew he was interested.

A few minutes later, I saw him walking towards the house down the sidewalk. I was ready for a break so I got back to take a look at the overall view. He was slightly taller than me and thin, but he had a wrestling team look to him. He hadn't shaved and was a bit older than I had thought, nearer twenty than 18.

"It's a hot day," he said as he walked by.

"I got started and bit off more than I can chew," I said. "It's looking better though."

"It looks good to me," the kid said. "Are you a gardener?"

"It's my Mom's house. Just visiting for a few days. She's out of town for a day or so and I decided to trim up the yard." He was pretending to look at the house, but was trying to look at me. I was sweating like a pig and my body hair was matted down with sweat. Sweaty, dirty and hairy, short men aren't just everybody's cup of tea, but once in a while, I look good to someone. This kid was almost drooling. I pretended not to notice. "Do you live nearby?" I asked.

"Three blocks away. I'm on summer break from college. My name is Jim."

"Pleased to meet you. They call me Clydesdale, that's short for Wildrige." He shook hands. There was a pause in the conversation. I realized he wasn't experienced in picking up men.

"I'm going in for some water, would you care to join me?" I said. The boy looked as if a Genie had granted his first wish. He said, 'sure'. "Let's go in the back door. I'm too dirty to cross the rugs." The kid looked around and saw that all the drapes and blinds of the neighbors' houses were pulled to keep out the sun. He looked relieved and then followed me to the rear.

When I was younger, I was one of those kids who played hard and got dirty. My Mom built an outdoor shower next to the utility room. It was open above, but screened from view. I told Jim I was going to clean up some and let him in the kitchen door. I went in and dropped my pants and hosed the worst of the dirt off. The clothes' washer was right under the utility room window, so I dropped the dirty clothes in and grabbed a towel.

Jim was inside and watching.

"Jim, would you like to shower? You look hot too," I said. He said 'no'. I got us some water and, as my eyes adjusted to the comparative darkness of the kitchen, I could see he had a hard on. He was trying to hide his erection and stare at my nearly naked body. I have never seen anyone as embarrassed. I didn't know what to do, but my cock solved the problem. It began to grow.

"Damn, you're a hairy guy," he said.

"Hairy and hung," I said. I pointedly looked at his crotch. "It looks as if you like that combination." I slipped my hand into his pants and stroked his cock. His cock head was already coated in pre cum. "Let's get naked and play some." I said as I slipped his shorts off. Jim was ready.

Jim was willing and able, but not well educated in the mysteries of man sex. We stood there naked and erect.

"What am I supposed to do?" he asked. I said, sucking cock was a good start. Jim looked afraid, excited and afraid. I decided to help him out and dropped to my knees and sucked his cock. It was as if he got an electric shock. After thirty seconds or so, he was a convert. I knew he was close to shooting, so I stopped and got up.

"Do you think you could do that to me?" I asked, he nodded and dropped to the floor. He looked at my cock good and hard. I could almost see him screwing up his courage.

"Take your time," I said. "If you don't want to do it, I understand. There are different strokes, for different folks." I could remember my first time. I wasn't sure what to do, or if I would like it. Horny and scared. Thinking back, I also remember how good it was, how relieved I was I had finally done it. I pulled the skin back exposing my head.

His lips finally touched my cock head and he relaxed after a few seconds of sucking. He was a natural and didn't have any problem with my dong. He stopped after a while and got up.

"I wasn't sure I could do it," he said. "I wanted to, but I wasn't sure."

"Did you like it?"

"It was better than I dreamed," Jim said. I suggested that we go to a bedroom and do it right. He didn't know what right meant, but he was game. He was tanned and muscular, with a patch of black hair in the middle of the chest and at his tits and a trail leading to his pubic bush. He had a nice cut cock and low hanging balls.

He liked sucking, but he loved the 69 position. We went at it hot and heavy. We had to slow down regularly, since he was so close to shooting. I told him I was getting revved up and I would tell him if I was close to shooting.

"What should I do?" Jim asked.

"Well, you either watch it shoot, or drink it up," I said. "It's up to you."

"You really eat it?" he said incredulously.

"I do, when I want to. It ain't piss, it's man seed, cock caviar. Some guys love it," I said. "Frankly, I don't think it tastes as good as precum. Yours is damn good. I love a guy who leaks nice and steady like you."

"You like it?"

"I surely do. You've tasted your own, haven't you?" He looked as if he were going to deny it, then admitted he had. "You liked it too, didn't you?" Jim nodded. I could tell he was real uneasy. He liked what he was doing, but was shocked he liked it.

"Jim, the biggest problem I had growing up was admitting I liked what I liked. I grew up here too. I was sure I was the only gay guy in the history of the town. The only guy in school who like cock, not pussy. As I got older, I finally admitted I was gay and that was fine. You don't have to screw pussy to be a good guy. Nothing in the Bible says, you have to fuck women to get to heaven. Who you sleep with has nothing to do with being a good man or woman."

"I don't know about it," Jim said.

"Let me tell you one thing that's for certain. I promise not to get pregnant!" I said. He laughed and sucked me again trying to swallowed my cock whole. I tried to warn me when I was ready to shoot, but was a bit late. He would have eaten every drop if he hadn't climaxed too. I'm not sure I had ever sucked a virgin shooting for the first time before. I will swear there was twenty years of backed up cum in that boy's balls. I had to swallow twice.

I guessed he would be done for a month after his orgasm, but Jim was still ready to go. It takes me 20 to 30 minutes to regroup after shooting. Jim may have been drained, but he wanted more. We talked for a while. I told him I was a former Policeman and had been a prison guard. He was a computer major at Tech, his Dad was a insurance agent. They had moved here a few years before and he had few friends.

Jim had been a geek in High School. He was on the track team and had done well, but only football and basketball counted. He had spent most of his time at the computer surfing. He had a summer job at the local Internet provider covering the modems at night.

"What is the name of the local company?" I asked.

"Sova.com," he said. "It small, but they know their stuff."

"Have you heard of eog.com?"

"How did you ever hear about that rinky dink operation?" he asked. "They tried to use our server. Don, the owner, wouldn't do it. They offered him good money for it too."

"What was wrong with them?"

"The original name of the website was Empire of God.com! They wanted to capitalize the 'E' and 'G' and told Don he would go to hell if he didn't capitalize God," Jim explained. "Don told them to go to hell and take Empire of God with them. They didn't seem to understand you can't redo the entire domain naming system for some religious freaks in Southern Virginia."

"Do you know who was associated with it and where they are?" I asked.

"I think they have their own server out towards Thomaston," Jim said. "It's in a trailer. Dr. Paul was there, he's a real nut case. A guy named Virgil and two computer nerds, Bert and Fred. I know the nerds. Don said, Bert was the biggest porn fancier in the county until he found God and became holier than the Pope. Fred's never been quite right. He was into guns and women. He was ugly as shit, dirty and pushing 400 pounds. He never got close to a woman, but he talks about the sanctity of the woman and the purity of Southern Womanhood."

"I'll bet he's substituted guns for a sex life," I said.

"Bert told me he has enough weapons to start World War III."

"You are friends with Bert?"

"Not really,... er sort of," Jim answered. "In a pinch, we borrow spare equipment from each other. They know their stuff technically. We help out in a pinch. Computer operations breakdown all the time and you need help pronto. Don wouldn't go near them, but he let me. Bert was actually helpful several times. Oh, that guy's name was Ovid, not Virgil. I took Latin and I got my poets mixed up."

Jim was getting hard again. I asked him what else he knew about the eog. com operation. I began to suck him while he talked. I played with his balls and began to sneak a finger back to his ass hole. He pretended his didn't notice, but he shifted his legs and ass so the path was clear.

"Bert says Fred's got a lot of weapons. He apparently started with World War II surplus. He was convinced the Russians were coming and he would hold them off single-handedly from his trailer. He's real trailer trash, but he actually bought a farm with a big house to hold his collection," Jim explained. "Once when Bert was a bit drunk, he told me, Fred had some big stuff. I assume big stuff was a bazooka, but he said it was still bigger. He didn't tell me what it is was."

Jim said, he wanted to suck me, so he stopped talking. I squeezed out a good sized bead of precum just before he started to suck. Jim stuck out his tongue and licked it as it quivered in the piss slit, right before he tried to swallow my entire cock. I'd never done a virgin before and was afraid it was too much for a first experience. Jim was okay with it. By the time the afternoon was over, he was a confirmed cock hound.

Part 9

"Hands up!" someone yelled. I almost had a heart attack, until I recognized Slim. Jim was shocked.

"You ass hole! Don't you know how to knock?" I asked. Slim was wearing his hat, holster, gun and nothing else.

"Jim, this is Slim. He's on our side, although I kind of hate to admit it!" I explained. "He's dumb as shit, but he loves cock, so at least he has one redeeming feature." Slim came in and immediately swallowed Jim's cock.

Slim was a good cock sucker. Jim was a forgiving kid and there is nothing like cock sucking to encourage forgiveness. Deep throating also seemed to hit the spot. Jim showed his appreciation when he shot another big load in the Deputy's mouth. I think Jim was a bit turned on by the Policeman. Being young is wonderful and Jim must have been twitching for a good minute and a half. Jim would be almost through when Slim would deep throat the kid's cock and Jim would muster another ejaculation.

I was pretty sure they would be seeing each other during the course of the summer vacation. After the orgasm we turned to business. Jim told Slim about the eog.com website. Slim knew Bert and Wally. They kept an eye on Wally whenever a notable appeared in the area. The State Police had him on a watch list in case the Governor, or a Senator appeared.

I soon discovered that Slim wasn't as dumb as he looked. He was so unimpressive and odd looking you wouldn't associate him with an investigation. He seemed to have a good knowledge of the "usual suspects", but also could tell the difference between an over aged cowboy and a real problem. Slim didn't think Wally was harmless. By contrast, he thought Bert was a follower, not a leader.

"Bert's just smart enough to be dangerous," Slim said. "He gets inspired and is enthusiastic, but never gets deep enough to know what he is really doing. He's the kind of guy who gets worked up over something he sees in the National Inquirer."

"Ovid," Slim said, "is another case. He's a good man who's gone bad. Some thing's wrong in his head. He had that nice wife and kids. It's the same situation as Buddy's wife. Somehow she changed her 100% all-American, Boy Scout husband into a depraved sinner." Slim paused. "I'm worried about Buddy's kids. It ain't safe there."

"What do you mean?" I asked.

"Bad vibes. I've got nothing to go on, but bad vibes," Slim said. "Anyone who talks as much as Dr. Paul does about the sanctity of motherhood and virginity and then breaks up as many families as he has, isn't kosher. There is something up."

"Do the women live near him?" I asked.

"They live in an abandoned trailer park about a mile away. The women call it the convent, but I have my doubts," Slim added.

"My younger sister knows one of the girls who lives there." Jim said. "They were best friends until the girl moved there. Dad thinks that the girl got too holy for us. Elsie thinks her friend is scared."

"I'd like to meet Dr. Paul," I said. "He sounds like a real piece of work."

"I think we might put off that pleasure until later," Slim said. "There may well be a situation when it would be good for you not to have met the worthy Divine."

"I'll ask Elsie to talk to her girl friend," Jim said.

"I don't want any amateur sleuthing," Slim cautioned. "This is a job for professionals." Slim and Jim both had to go, so I returned to the yard and finished my pruning.

Mr. Edland died that evening. Earl had a murder on his hands, but he played his cards close to his chest. Remarkably, those who knew about the tampered brakes kept it to themselves. The rest of the town was unaware of the circumstances of the teacher's death. Mom returned as soon as she found out. She didn't want me to do anymore investigating.

"Mom, I told him I'd do the fighting this time," I said.

"Clydesdale. The Sheriff is a smart man," she said. "He has everything under control. You know Earl hates a murder on his turf. It just offends him. You work on the Richmond end, he'll do the Victoriaville angle." She was right. I didn't have the connections I used to. And, while I'm not prone to admire any one other than my own policing, I had a feeling he and Slim were good. I would be more useful in Richmond.

I didn't go the funeral. Mom said, since Mr. Edland and I had not been on the best of terms in High School, it might look odd. "Plus," she said, "the murderer will be there. He doesn't need to see you. I'll give you a report." I went back to Richmond after I gave Earl all my information and suppositions. Earl was thinking the same way I was. He had people planted in the church to find out what was going on.

Richmond was quiet. The investigation had reached the pure slogging phase of work. The computer nerds were refining their search of the web and seemed to find increasing confirmation of the eog.com connection to the bombing. Most weird and wacko sites have a limited attention span, but not the eog.com site. It was still talking about God's judgment and justice wreaked upon the godless infidels of Richmond.

The laboratory studies had all but ruled out foreign involvement. It didn't fit the patterns of any known terrorist groups. It was an original M.O., home made, rather than imported.

I went to the bombing site and the area was a beehive of activity. All the debris was gone and minor repairs were well under way. The big damage remained. One side of the temple was gone and temporary shoring supported the dome. Blue tarps were everywhere. You couldn't fit another carpenter's pickup on the neighboring streets if you wanted too. Some people who had seemed to be in shock after the bombing were cleaning and fixing. I think activity can heal. You feel better if you are doing something. It amazed me at how fast people recovered from such a major disaster.

It was Friday. The Temple services were being held in a neighboring church. It had plywood in place of glass, but was otherwise undamaged. We provided security, but there was a very heavy Richmond Police presence. We were undercover, looking for potential problems, assuming the bombers would avoid the uniformed Police. We also provided security for three other temples and a school.

The City administration wasn't enthusiastic about the bombing investigation, but the individual members of the Police and Fire Departments were. They wanted to get the guys as badly as we did. I ran into John, the contractor, and Max, the architect, inspecting the work. They were trying to get the repairs done as quickly as possible, but had run into problems with the Building Code people. The street was all offices and apartments, other than the churches and the Temple. The Mayor was blocking repairs because he wanted it to be a street of single family homes.

He said, he wanted it to be a wholesome street, that seemed to exclude the Gay newspaper and the Women's Health Clinic. Eleanor Salina and Ari were there. She was rip roaring mad and not in a mood to take prisoners. Her house had only lost its windows in the blast, but her neighbor's house across the street was badly burned out. The mayor had stopped all permits until the land use question was resolved and her neighbors were frantic to save what was left and get back in their houses. Blue tarps only last so long.

The neighborhood was inhabited by professional people and Eleanor figured she would mobilize some lawyers. Max said, the mayor didn't have a leg to stand on, but he was afraid if it hit the courts the whole process could go on forever. Eleanor and Max went off to plot strategy. She also was to appear at a big memorial service in the Cathedral on Sunday. The local Clergy wanted to show solidarity with the Temple so the service was at the biggest church in the area. I realized the general assumption still was the bombing was anti-Semitic.

John asked me, to come over for dinner the next night. He was having some friends over. I was going to say 'No', I was too busy, but I said 'Yes'. I hadn't done anything not work related in a while. Except for sex with emergency workers, policemen or leads in the case, of course.

The next day I spent interviewing new employees. We were growing and I didn't want to have unqualified guys on the job. Butch had done some preliminary interviews, but he felt I had a nose for trouble. I agreed with him on that. I can smell a bullshit artist a mile away.

It was a productive day. I found several good men. We did real well with retired police and military men. These men were already trained, but they really appreciated working in a place where they didn't have to hide their sexual interests. I hired one oddball. Lonnie was a former waiter, chef, locker room attendant and florist.

Lonnie looked macho enough, but he was a few steps to the right side of Pee Wee Herman in terms of masculinity, but only a few. He told me he was the last person in the world anyone would suspect of being a detective. He moved in Richmond's swishy circles and was totally harmless as far as anyone would guess. I could see where he would be helpful.

I went over to John's house for dinner. His firm, Millennium Construction, had outgrown his house, so he had moved his offices out of the first floor into a bigger building. It was a shock to see living room furniture in place in the parlors. The murals of nude Confederate Generals were well displayed. I remembered the stir they caused when John uncovered them a year earlier. The nude Lee remained my favorite.

I was there a little late, most of my friends from Clydesdale & Company and Millennium Construction were already there as well as Vince and Ari. I got a beer and talked. The room was crowded. The sliding doors to the dining room were closed. I assumed John hadn't had time to decorate the other rooms on the first floor. I was talking with Tom and Ed, John's right-hand men, when a gong sounded.

Skeeter and John came down the stairs, wearing top hats.

"Welcome gentlemen and not quite gentlemen!" John announced grandly. "Tonight we have the great unveiling of my new dining room, just redecorated and restored. Ari has catered the event with my neighbors Karl and Bob."

Karl, John's next door neighbor and a caterer appeared wearing a chef's hat. "This is a new breakthrough in the world of Richmond catering." he proclaimed. "We have managed to combine Nouvelle Cuisine with Homo Baroque decoration to create a new style." Karl and Skeeter pushed the big sliding doors open.

The Dining room was illuminated with a spectacular chandelier, in the center of the dining room table was a huge ice sculpture of a cock. The room burst into laughter. The room was really beautiful and the contrast between its elegance and the ice cock was outrageous. The entire table was filled with cock like or ball like food. Some erect, some semi erect and the Brie dick had already melted. There was a huge, three tiered birthday cake in the corner.

"Oh shit!" I said. The cake was inscribed "Happy Birthday Clydesdale!" The room burst into laughter again. Everyone began singing, "Happy Birthday to You" and the top of the cake began to move.

I think Mark was supposed to jump out of the cake, but such feats of athletic prowess weren't his cup of tea. He did eventually get out of the cake and he made up for the clumsiness by being stark naked. Everyone was laughing so hard it really didn't make any difference.

I was showered with gifts. "You guys must think I like nothing but sex!" I said after getting my third bottle of lube and sixth bottle of poppers.

"Only when you're awake!" Mark said. I guess he had a point. Dinner looked odd, but tasted good. I had a good time and everyone was in a good mood. The mood got even better when John broke out the Viagra and gave it to those who wanted it. Mark never got dressed. Skeeter, Ram and Vince joined him. They were all well hung and their big dicks seemed to inspire just about everyone.

Skeeter let us know his attic bedroom was the playroom. He called it the "fuck pen". The guest room on the second floor was christened the "suckatorium". I had wondered how many guys at the party would take advantage of a playroom. There was no pressure to go upstairs, but, at this party at least, everyone was interested.

Above the first floor everyone was naked. I wandered up there around eight and got an opportunity to use some of the Treasure-Trove of "marital aids." I put the poppers away. With the Viagra, there were enough chemicals in our bodies. I also figured dildos were like carrying coals to Newcastle. There were enough real cocks to make dildos unnecessary. Some of the lube was really good.

Skeeter was famous as a cock sucker and cum hound. He set up shop in the "suckatorium". Bobby, a diminutive laborer who worked for John, was a confirmed bottom and he was the lube master for the attic. Bobby was sitting on the stair at the attic entrance and lubricating everyone's ass hole as they went in the room.

Bobby knew his way around an ass and his little fingers got your entire tunnel slicked up in no time. I don't know exactly what he did, but he poked my prostate a few times and seemed to have tripped my "on" button. Mark was right behind me and received the same treatment.

"Hot damn! You're good!" he said to Bobby. He had never met Bobby before. Bobby was looking at Mark, eye to cock.

"You got a keeper there!" Bobby said appreciatively. He poked Mark's prostate a few times to inflate Mark's donkey dong to full erection. "It's a beauty."

"It works for me." Mark said.

"Do you give rides?" asked Bobby.

"I sure do, but aren't your eye's bigger than your ass?" replied Mark. "You'd make a real nice hood ornament, but I'd hate to split you in half."

"Let me be the judge of that," Bobby said. "Take a seat." Bobby coated Mark's dick and when Mark sat on the top step, Bobby got up, positioned Mark's cock at his hole and sat back. There was no hesitation, the entire cock slipped in as if Bobby's ass was designed for it. Bobby arched his back once the whole cock was in. He shivered a few times and wiggled his ass to get more comfortable. I had to admit they both looked happy.

Skeeter's attic apartment was quiet. Vince was there fucking Larry. Vince had a hard time finding guys who could take his man rammer. John told me, Larry wasn't normally a bottom, he only did it for Vince. I guess if you're going to become a bottom, you might as well start at the top!

John and Ed were on the bed. Ed waved me over so I joined them. I had a suspicion they were waiting for me.

Part 10

I'd spent so much time out of town recently, I had neglected my old friends. John had a special relationship with my cock. John and I were good friends, he was a nice guy and the original financial support for Clydesdale & Company. His ass was in love with my cock. They fit perfectly and my dong rang a bell no one else had ever rung.

Some people might say I am obsessively sex driven. I admit I get my share of sex. John wasn't a sex maniac. I think he was embarrassed, at first, at his reaction to my cock. He told me he never totally lost control the way he did when my cock head rammed his prostate. It's hard for a middle-aged businessman to admit a redneck cock drove him crazy.

John was used to it now and could relax and let my cock work its magic. It wasn't as good for me as for him, but it was nice to be appreciated. I'm not sure I understood what he felt until I ran in to Mark. Actually, it would be more correct to say I didn't understand until Mark's cock ran in to my prostate.

At this very moment, Bobby was bouncing up and down on Mark's cock on the stairs, so I took advantage of John's quivering and welcoming ass. John was on the bed with his legs spread, so I slipped right in. John's best friend, Ed, was watching.

"Damn, that looks easy!" Ed said. "I'm not sure I've seen a big one slip in so smooth."

"John makes it that way," I said, "He really likes it." I gave him a few quick thrusts and John moaned.

"I've never had much luck with big ones," Ed said. "Nice to look at and inspirational, but hard to take."

"You're nicely equipped yourself," I said. Ed had a good cock, but Ed himself was real attractive. He wasn't pretty. He was handsome, manly I guess you would say. A bit stocky, with blond hair turning white, he was muscular from hard work rather than the gym. He had a white beard and was covered in curly white body hair. Someone had described him as a blond Bluto. Unlike Bluto, he was affable, smart and organized. He was John's right hand man.

He was like John in that he wasn't sex driven, like me. Ed liked sex, but he didn't get carried away. Both men were builders. They got the excitement and thrill I get from catching a criminal; Ed got it by building something. I think Max, the Architect, felt the same way. Even though I like sex a lot, I have always thought of it as a sideline. I've met some guys who were professional gays. It never seemed to me being gay was your day job. Men need to do something real.

I did get the distinct feeling sex was on Ed's mind now and the sex he was thinking about involved me. The room was quiet, except for heavy breathing and Larry's moans. Vince had him right on the edge of an orgasm, but had managed to keep him teetering on the edge. Larry was whimpering to finish him off, he couldn't stand it anymore. Vince didn't get to top that often and wasn't going to stop until he was good and ready.

"Have you ever been there?" I asked Ed, referring to Larry.

"No, not really," Ed said. "I got my wife there a few times, but I shoot too easy to be there myself."

"When did you change over to men?" I asked.

"After she died," he said. "At first I thought it was because there were fewer strings attached to men. When I hit fifty, I admitted the sex was better."

"Never got married myself," I said, while giving John a few deep strokes with my cock. "I liked men from the start. When you look like me, it's not as if there's a line of women lusting after your bod. It was easy for me. No one expected me to get married."

"You do better with men?" Ed asked. He was smiling.

"I sure do," I replied. "Even straight men respond when you are hung like the Statue of Liberty's stud muffin." I pulled my cock entirely out of John's ass. The lubricant glistened and emphasized every vein on my shaft. I shoved it back in hard. John gasped for breath. He liked that a lot.

"I use to get guys who were curious. They wanted to feel it and sometimes suck it," I continued. "The real brave ones wanted it in the ass. I'm afraid I'm more than willing to accommodate them."

"John told me it was an incredible sensation," Ed said. "He wasn't sure men were meant to feel the way it made him feel." I gave John a few more thrusts and cum spurted from his cock, hands free. The sperm made graceful arcs over his gut and landed on his hairy chest. It was a top of the line orgasm and John was all but asleep by the time it was over, drained. I pulled out.

Ed and I were on the bed next to John. I stroked Ed's hard cock. His cock head was covered in precum.

"You liked watching, didn't you?" I asked.

"I guess I did," he said sheepishly. "I'm kind of embarrassed, but I did."

"More turned on then embarrassed?"

"Yep," he said.

"There is nothing wrong with watching guys enjoy themselves," I said.

"There sure isn't!" Mark added. He had finished on the stairs with Bobby and joined us. "That Bobby is a wonder. "Takes a licking and keeps on ticking." I've never screwed anyone that small. I was afraid my cock would stick out of his mouth, but it didn't." Ed and I laughed. "Are you hunting for big meat?" he asked of Ed.

"Damn, Mark. You are so refined!" I said. "Here Ed and I were having this nice conversation and you butt in."

"As a matter of fact, I was thinking about sampling big meat," Ed said, smiling. "I figured this was the right place to find it. It looks like I'm a bit oversupplied with dick, a surfeit of cock."

"You got one real inviting cock," Mark said. He was looking at Ed's hard and dripping dick. "I love them juicy!" he added. Mark climbed on the bed, straddled Ed's cock and sat on it. This caught me by surprise. Mark usually tops.

"Shit, that's good," Ed said. He was surprised too, but enjoyed it. Mark had been at half staff when he took the cock. His meat looked as if it was a balloon filled with helium. He was doing a version of a hula on Ed's love pole, trying to get the maximum sensation from Ed's cock. From the look on his face, Mark liked it more than he expected.

"Do you mind if I get off before I pop?" Mark asked.

"No problem," Ed replied. "I'd like some more playtime before I drop my first load." Mark got up.

"Anytime you need an ass to keep your cock warm, give me a call!" Mark said. "Damn, that was good." Ed looked at me and I knew he was thinking about my cock and his ass. John was awake, looked at me and got a tube of lubricant off of the table next to the bed. John got up and Ed spread his legs. John began to work some lube into Ed's ass. He also squirted some on my cock.

Ed's pink ass hole was pretty, with a little rosebud peeking out. His cock was rock hard and still dripping and his balls were pulled tight. I knew he was as ready as he ever would be. I rested my cock head at his ass and my piss slit touched his rosebud. I pushed. He resisted. John opened a bottle of Rush and gave Ed a good snort.

A second later my cock was in. Ed's ass all but swallowed my cock whole. He gasped for air as if he were winded. I was a bit uneasy. I never ram my cock in full depth, unless I know the guy real well and know he likes it that way. I just stood there with my pubic hair pressed against his hole and my dick in, as deep as it could get.

"Holy shit!" he exclaimed. Ed's ass twitched, then he wiggled a bit to get a more comfortable fit. I felt better. I pulled out a little, then went back in deep. I did this a few times, until I was sure he was enjoying it. Then we got down to real fucking. As I said, I'm a careful guy when it comes to fucking. I like to make sure my partner likes it as much as me. That can be a challenge with a cock as big as mine.

It didn't take me long to realize Ed liked it a bit rough. He wanted me to pull my cock out, then ram him to the hilt as fast and hard as I could. I can be really fast and my cock was really hard. That was fine with Ed. John seemed to enjoy watching Ed have a good time. Ed was usually reserved, but you can't hold back when my cock is playing tag with your prostate.

The room was quiet. Vince had filled Larry's ass and Larry was resting. Bobby looked as if he was a wet dishrag. He had huge orgasms, and afterward, Bobby was usually drained. Vince came over and touched me on the shoulder.

"May I cut in?" he asked. I moved out of the way and he slipped his cock into Ed's ass. Mark motioned to me to get on the bed. Mark was usually physically ungainly, but he got my legs on his shoulder and his cock in my ass in a single graceful movement. His cock sent me to the moon on the first thrust. After fifteen minutes of hard work, we were both happy.

It turned out to be a good night. Normally a climax like the one I had with Mark was enough to put me out of commission for a good hour. I think the Viagra may have been inspirational. I was interested in sex in ten minutes and ready to screw in fifteen.

Since it was my birthday party, several guys came to me to get a inaugural ride on my cock. Otto, John's somewhat swishy painter, was a real find. He wasn't a virgin and took my cock like a pro. Swishy isn't my favorite flavor of fag, but he was good. Otto must have had some muscles in his shit chute lacking in most men. It was like one of those electric massage heating pads, hot and quivering.

At first Otto was just being polite and perhaps a bit curious. After about three minutes, he was a lot more than polite. Lance, Otto's partner in work and love, also joined in. He fed Otto his cock, while I plugged his lover's ass.

Karl and Bob, John's next door neighbors, also made the big jump. Bob was a top and Karl had decided I would be the perfect introduction to the science of being a bottom. I don't know how that happened, but I had a suspicion Bob had lost a bet and my cock was the punishment. Karl was a professional caterer and semi-professional bottom. He was going to be the coach.

We were watching Vince pounding Bobby when Bob whispered in my ear, he would like to give it a try. Bobby was the 'poster boy' for anal sex. He loved it and seemed to never get enough of it. Mark had fucked him earlier and that only seemed to increase Bobby's desire for monster meat. He was spread eagled on the bed with his ass wide open and Vince was deep fucking him.

One of the nice added attractions to having a big cock is the view it gives onlookers. Vince was proud of his mighty dong and he pulled the entire thing out on each thrust, giving us a good view. The coating of lubricant made his cock look like it had been candied. The glistening ointment showed every inch of his cock in great detail. Bobby was small and you could see him react to each thrust. It was like a Keystone Cops routine, except it was to see how much cock you could fit into a single ass rather than cops into an antique car.

Bobby was in heaven. He liked it and everyone knew. Bob was inspired. We went over to the bed and Bob bent over. Karl lubed him up and had all but his thumb in Bob's ass. Karl showed no mercy and Bob didn't seem to mind. Bob was handsome, almost pretty. Every hair was always in place and I felt kind of odd shoving my cock in his ass. No Greek sculptor would have immortalized my cock. What it lacks in beauty it makes up for in size.

I did him doggy style. My cock slipped in easily enough, but there were no fireworks. Bob wasn't in pain, but he wasn't enjoying it either. Karl wandered away.

"This isn't working, is it?" I asked.

"It's not bad." Bob said. "It must not do for me what it does for Bobby, or Karl for that matter."

"Want to try it spread eagled?" I asked. "Sometimes another position feels better. Usually doggy style is easiest to take, but you never know." Bob agreed. I pulled out and he got on the bed. I lifted his legs and repositioned my cock. Bobby was free from Vince's cock and squirted my cock with additional lubricant.

The minute my cock head cleared the sphincter, I knew this was the way to go. Bob twitched and shivered the whole way. By the time I was in deep, he had a spectacular hard and was moaning. Apparently my cock hit every good spot in his ass. It felt so good, he involuntarily spasmed. After two or three deep thrusts, I had figured out what to do to drive him crazy and Bob had lost it.

Karl returned and was inspired himself. He wanted to replace me in his lover's ass. I figured he had the right, so I let him. Karl was better hung than I remembered. I am often surprised to find guys, who aren't my type, can still have some heavy meat. Karl was a bottom and didn't seem to have much technique as a top. He just shoved it in and didn't seek out the good spots.

I took charge and slowed him down and gave him some guidance. When I got him to concentrate on one of Bob's good spots, Karl finally got the idea. He got Bob's legs on his shoulders and had bent Bob back, so they could kiss. Bob was a lot more flexible than I am. This move left Karl's hole wide open. His rosebud was peaking out. I was trying to decide what to do next, when Karl's ass winked at me.

I coated my cock with lubricant again and slipped into the welcoming ass. I had fucked Karl once before, but he was concentrating on Bob, so he just opened up and let me in. His entire fuck tunnel was contracting as he began to ejaculate. I kept on pumping, so his ejaculatory spasms massaged my cock. It was great. I was right on the edge of shooting when I pulled out.

I was a bit lost, when Bobby came up to me.

"It's your turn!" he said. "I've got three loads in there already, you won't need no lube." Bobby was right about that. Man seed is a great lubricant.

Part II

When my cock slipped into Bobby's waiting ass, Mark's and Vince's cum oozed out of the tight space between my rock hard cock and Bobby's stretched ass hole. It was like when you bite into a cream filled donut and the cream spurts out. Bobby had been royally fucked twice, but was just as enthusiastic with me in his ass.

Bobby didn't mind a little mess, when it comes to fucking. There was cum, precum and ass juices, all intermingled in his ass. I think his hole might have been tight a few hours before. He had been tenderized and by this time, he was wide open. The inside of his chute was hot and juicy. My cock floated on a sea of cum. Butch and Bubba joined me. What we were doing looked good to them, so we all shared his ass. As soon as I got ready to shoot, I would pull out and let one of them replace me. We would trade off and Bobby was in a perpetual motion fucking machine. Bobby was in heaven, as he was continuously fucked for a half hour by the three of us.

Eventually, I miscalculated and began to cum. I pulled out of Bobby's ass and much to my surprise, found Skeeter sucking my load straight from the spigot. Skeeter is a cum hound. Butch and Bubba shot off in Bobby's ass. When Bubba finished, Skeeter took his place, holding Bobby's legs open for another fucking. I thought Skeeter was going to take up topping. He didn't. He got on his knees and rimmed Bobby while holding Bobby's legs open. As the cum oozed from the ravaged hole, Skeeter lapped it up.

Skeeter was almost tender in the way he licked the man seed as it emerged. It was a cum hounds dream come true. I was beside Skeeter and stroked his cock as he licked. I had never seen him so hard. It only took a few stokes to make him cum, but he never lost a lick, even during his orgasm.

I may never win the Mother Theresa's Award for service to humanity, but teaching Karl how to fuck his lover Bob was a real service. They had been together for years and this new expanded repertoire of sex acts, changed their lives for the good. They both loved it. Actually, the perpetual motion fucking machine was a good idea too.

After a night like that, you would think the next day would be a let down. This was the day of the big memorial service at the Cathedral. There was a march from the outlying churches in the neighborhood to the Cathedral, where there would be a city wide service. I was up early, when I got a call from Elinor. She said, there was no police protection for the march and service.

Usually the city blankets a district with police whenever there is a march, or parade. I called the Police Headquarters and asked what was up. They said the parade and service weren't official city functions, so there was going to be no police presence. This was a newly minted policy from the Mayor's office. I told the dispatcher that most of the fucking dead were police and fire personnel. She hung up on me. I called Butch, Roosevelt, Fred and Vince. They raced to the office. Vince made a few calls and got the Police Union to call their members and get off duty officers on the scene. He got the fire department to do the same. At least there would be some uniformed men in attendance.

Fifteen minutes later Earl called.

"Clydesdale. Slim called and said there was a late night meeting at Wally's house. Slim passed the house accidentally and saw them load up a Van with boxes. It was about three in the morning and they took off," the sheriff said. "He followed them to Richmond. They're in a Brown GMC van. Wally, Ovid and Bert were in the van with another guy Slim didn't recognize. Slim was off duty so didn't have a radio or cell phone. He lost them when he called me from a 7-11."

"Did he know where they were headed?"

"Toward downtown," Earl said. I told Earl to give Slim my number and we could outfit him with all the communication devices he needed.

"What is the license number?" I asked.

"Obscured," Earl said. "Covered in mud. It's a '94 GMC van."

"How many boxes?"

"Six, normal sized, packing boxes. They were carrying them as if they were heavy," Earl said. He hung up.

Guys were beginning to show up at our office. Our Internet man reported, the sickos were writing about false prophets and false religion. That was a bad sign. We alerted everyone to look out for a Van. I wanted to get out and start looking. Butch and Vince were the organizational types. I'm a field man. I took a group of our men over to the march site and we began to sweep the area for suspicious persons and objects.

A half hour later Butch drove by and gave me a dog. Killerpoo was the oddest animal I had ever seen. It must have been a Cock-a-Poo-Bassett mix. He was a bomb sniffer replacement for Roger, who had been killed at the bombing. The dog was half nose and half cock. He was very friendly. I got a radio message the van was at the Science Museum, three blocks away. I raced over there.

When I got there, Slim was waiting. He had found it. It was locked, the mud on the plates was paint. It took about a minute to get in the van. Killerpoo went bonkers the minute he sniffed the interior. There had been explosives in the van. I ran to my car and called 911, telling them there was a probable bombing in the works. That got their attention. The men had left a jacket in the Van. Slim gave Killerpoo a sniff and the mutt was off. Police cars, fire trucks and EMS trucks began to converge on the site. The dog cared for nothing but the scent.

I was racing after Slim and Killerpoo. There apparently was a very clear scent and the dog was a tracking wonder. Three minutes later, the dog stopped at a trash can. He went crazy again. It was in a narrow alley, between the closely packed houses along the route of the march. I called the police and told them where we were. An ATF Van arrived in a minute and a half. Killerpoo wasn't finished yet. The trail continued.

Three blocks away we found another box. This was shoved under a pick up truck. That truck was parked in front of a big Presbyterian church, also on the line of the march. The city Police arrived for that one. I called the office and told them I thought the bombs were placed along the march route. We were following one of the bombers, but there were three other men possibly dispensing bombs.

A reporter and camera crew from a local station intercepted us. Slim gave them a quick and concise description of the men. He said, we had found two bombs and there were at least four more. All were in plain brown boxes. He said, he guessed they were set to go off in an hour or so, to explode during the march. I was off on the hunt with Killerpoo and two of our operatives.

I found out later that Roosevelt was interviewed after Slim and said, people should look over their own property to see if there were any boxes around. This was a big city neighborhood, maybe twenty thousand people. A minute after the live report, a good ten thousand of them must have gone out looking.

A group of college students captured Wally. He wouldn't tell them anything about the bombs, but they changed his mind for him. One of the students later told the television his knife accidentally slipped and cut off one of Wally's fingers. Wally understood the lay of the land and he told them the bombs were set to go off at one fifteen, there were only six bombs and there was no radio control. He also told them where he planted a bomb.

A group of enraged neighbors captured Bert. He was trying to vanish into a group of Presbyterians as they fled from their church. It was evacuated after we discovered the bomb in the front yard. He apparently was as unconvincing as a Presbyterian as a man could be. Sporting a dirty tee shirt, jeans and having a furtive look, is not the way to blend into an upscale Protestant population.

You would think it would be better to be captured by the Presbyterians and their neighbors than the College students. Bert didn't need to have any fingers sewed back on at least, but Bert clearly knew the error of his ways by the time the police took custody, or more correctly, rescued him. There were still two bombers and two bombs missing.

Killerpoo was still game, so apparently our bomber was still at large. The trail went down the street toward the Cathedral, past the bombed Temple. We had 24 hour security at the bombed Temple area, so there were no bombs there. The students had found a second bomb in the park, across the street from the Cathedral. There was a six-block gap between the bombs. Killerpoo took a left turn and went away from the march site. One bomb and two bombers were missing.

We raced across streets and through alleys. Ahead was a Hardee's with Ovid, sitting under an umbrella, drinking a coke with a brown box on the seat next to him. We arrested him.

"You can't arrest me!" he said. "I'm doing God's work."

"What a fucking asshole!" Ellen said. Ellen was our token lesbian and as hard as nails. I couldn't have said it better myself.

"We have Wally and Burt. Who is the fourth man?" I asked.

"There isn't a fourth man," Ovid said. Ellen smacked him in the balls. Ovid turned white.

"Tell the nice man what he wants to know," Ellen said. "We got no time for polite chitchat." She got ready to smack him again.

"It's Sally. She had to prove herself," Ovid said. Sally was Buddy's wife.

"Shit," I said. The Police arrived and we didn't have a chance to question him anymore. Ovid tried to claim police brutality, but none of the eyewitnesses saw anything, including me. As soon as I could, I called Buddy and told him to go to a judge and get his kids. There was big trouble. I called Mom and Earl too. Earl had warrants and court orders ready and was ready to rescue the children and search the Victory Temple.

The whole thing was covered live on national television, so everyone knew what was going on. Slim and Killerpoo were heroes and three of the bombers were captured. There was no direct evidence against the Victory Temple itself, or the preacher who was behind it. It was non-stop interviews and reports for the next six hours. The march was postponed to four in the afternoon. 100,000 people came to it and it went off without an incident.

It was a great success, but I was worried. We had all the bombs and three of the bombers. Sally had escaped and there was no way to guess the mental state of a rural house wife turned terrorist. She was obviously off the deep end.

Elinor gave a great speech, reaffirming real American values of tolerance and openness. The Bishop gave a brief sermon on why Jesus didn't use a bomb. I got back to my apartment at 9:00, exhausted, but too tired to go to bed.

I tried to call my Mom, but she wasn't home. I guessed she was with cousin Buddy and his kids. Mark showed up with two six packs. That hit the spot. We sat back and watched cable news. At 10:30 the phone rang. It was Mom, the kids were safe. They had been locked up in a trailer to "protect" them from the evils of the world. They were malnourished, but fine. Mom was taking care of the malnourished problem. Buddy was a nice guy, but not a cook. She had been cooking for the last few hours and was going back the next morning to get Buddy's house "regular".

"You did well dear," she said. "We saw it all on the TV." She paused. "They are the small fry, aren't they?"

"That would be my guess, Mom."

"Do you think Wally and his crew will incriminate the Preacher," she asked.

"I don't know. If I was doing the questioning they would," I said.

"I assume he's protected himself. That kind always do," Mom said. "Your Aunts Becky and Ellen are here. We agreed if we were doing the questioning, we would get to the bottom of it too."

"Thumbscrews and the rack?" I asked laughing.

"We are dealing with a murderous maniac here. He finds weak people and has them do his dirty work," Mom said, seriously. "You be careful, but he must be stopped." She hung up.

There was an edge I heard in her voice. She was worried about something. I would call Earl in the morning and get a fuller version of the goings on at home. Mark was ready for bed. I was too tired for sex I thought.

I got in bed and Mark got in with me. He started sucking and wanted to 69. That was difficult, because he was so much taller than me. I gave it a try and his cock and tongue worked their magic. I fell asleep after a climax and woke up the next morning with him still sucking. I don't know if he sucked all night.

I sucked him to full erection. I got him close several times, then sat on his cock. You really feel close to a guy when he has 10 inches of cock in your ass. I spent a good fifteen minutes twitching and squirming on his love pole until he popped and rear loaded me. I fell asleep again with his cock still in my ass. When I woke at 7:00 he was making breakfast. It was a real breakfast, all eggs and bacon. We were sitting naked at the breakfast table, when Butch and Roosevelt came upstairs from the office below.

"You boys been playing?" Butch asked.

"We sure have. Cum is a great sleeping potion," Mark replied. "It's a good waker upper too."

"I used a damn alarm clock!" Roosevelt said. "Would you like a quick roll in the hay, or are too bushed to play?" Butch was already unbuttoning his shirt, so I guess he anticipated our reply. Roosevelt was unzipping.

"I need to think some about that," Mark said. He wasn't very convincing as his cock was already well beyond half staff. "I've never tried dark meat before," Roosevelt had his cock out by this time. It was impressive. Mark smiled as he looked at the large dong. "I guess I might as well try it. At least I'm starting at the top." Roosevelt laughed.

"Don't worry White Boy! My cum is as white as yours!" I was 69ing with Butch and we left Mark and Roosevelt alone to get acquainted. Roosevelt is a real handsome man, gym fit and well groomed. Mark is kind of goofy looking. He looked as if he never combed his hair, but possessed a monster, uncut dick of a good 8 to 9 inches. I didn't think Mark was Roosevelt's type, but big dicks can make friends fast, if you have that taste. Roosevelt obviously did.

I lost track of things when Butch's cock began to ooze big time. This morning his precum was almost intoxicating. When I looked up the next time, Mark was easing his cock into Roosevelt's chute. I thought Roo was a top, but Mark's cock must have inspired him. Butch and I went over to help them out.

I knew Butch and Roosevelt were lovers. They were both handsome, very macho men. Roosevelt craved monster cocks and Butch was only above average. I was worried at first, but realized Mark had the cock Roosevelt liked, but nothing else. It was pure sex and curiosity and Mark was no threat to Butch's relationship with Roosevelt. Several weeks later Butch told me Roosevelt had mentioned Mark's dick and admired it. Our meeting this morning wasn't accidental.

Mark is no brain surgeon material, but he must have sensed Roosevelt's ass wasn't experienced. He was careful and tender as he worked it in.

"Relax baby. You can take it all!" Butch said to Roosevelt as he caressed the black man's sweating brow. "It hurts now but you'll love it when the whole thing is in all the way." Roosevelt was sweating like a pig and shivering as Mark relentlessly worked his cock deep into the quivering tunnel. I guessed they were "no pain, no gain" men and they liked the struggle to fit the cock in Roosevelt's ass.

Roosevelt's cock was rock hard and pointing up, dribbling precum. I licked it and cleaned his cock head. More oozed as soon as I finished. I licked that up too, then kissed Butch. That turned Butch on big time. He leaned over to get some of Roosevelt's cock cream for himself and I took the opportunity to ease my cock into his ass. Both Butch and Roosevelt were normally tops, but they were in a bottom mood this morning.

Butch arranged himself, so that Roosevelt could suck him while he was sucking Roosevelt. Butch normally fought an intruder in his ass, but not this time. There was no resistance as my dick rammed his prostate. Roosevelt had a front row, center view of that and must have been inspired. Mark let out a sigh of satisfaction as the last three inches of his cock lodged in the black man's ass.

He stood still for a while, than began pumping. We double teamed them. When Mark was in, I was pulling out. We built up speed and all four of us popped within a minute. It was good. The phone rang. It was Earl. There was more trouble at the Victory Temple.

Part 12

Sally was missing and Ovid, Wayne and Bert, sat in jail. I think my own interrogation techniques would have speeded things up considerably. My lesbo officer could have found out anything we needed and made sure the bastards never had any kids, to boot. This is America and we can't do that.

I got a visit from one of my old friends on the force, Captain Londry. He said, they needed some inside the jail information. He had a suspicion the men would brag about their achievements if given a chance.

"There is something smug about them, they have that sanctimonious look that drives me up the wall. They are fucking proud about what they did and would jump at a chance to tell someone to bask in the glory!" the Captain said. I knew he was riled. He never used profanity in day to day life. It took something special.

"We need someone who would never be suspected of being a cop," Londry continued. "No offense, but you came to mind immediately." I laughed. He had often complained about my lack of Police-like authority.

"I know Ovid," I said.

"We know that, I talked to Sheriff Earl." Londry said. "Each is in solitary, they can't talk to each other at all. Wayne is the brains behind it, we think and I'm not sure he would fall for it. Bert is the man for us. You don't know him, do you?"

"Not at all." I said.

"They are in solitary, but in two-man cells. We're going to feed him a line about overcrowding and a need to double up," Londry said. "I think a firearms violation would do the trick. Do you think you could be a member in good stand of a gun running ring?"

"I kind of think I can," I said. "I sure got the look. He didn't see my picture with the kids at the bombing?"

"Have you looked in the mirror lately? You don't look the way you did at the time of the bombing. Your new haircut is a wonder. And you do have the look of a gun runner," the Captain said. I was in jail that night. I had been a prison guard and I ran into some old playmates manning the gates. They told me to be free and easy about what I did in the cell. They would only interrupt if I needed help. I said, it was more likely he would need the help.

"It's amazing how guys get hurt in a prison, pure accidental like," my old friend, Ed, said. "Don't do it unless you need to, but if you need a witness who can swear on a stack of Bibles it was an accident, I'm your man. If you have time, after you're done, you could drop by my apartment and we could talk about old times?"

I grabbed his crotch and told him, "Sure. Are any of the old gang around?"

"Yep, Carter and Chuck bunk with me," Ed said.

"Hot damn!" I said. "I'd love a reunion." With that information, I got to the cell and became Bert's cell mate.

Bert wasn't what I thought he would be. I had guessed smart ass, but hadn't dreamed he was both dumb and a know it all. I also hadn't guessed he was good looking. He had been pumping iron and had boyish good looks. The cell was hot and he was stripped to the waist. He had a shaved head and must have shaved the rest of his body too. He wasn't an outdoors man and was white, with delicate pink tits.

He was surly and rude until he discovered my crime. I told him I was smuggling guns. I went into a tirade against the Feds and the Constitution and threw in a few comments about the UN and black helicopters. Bert knew an intellectual when he met one. An hour later we were best friends and he was filling me in on all his deepest thoughts. We were sitting on our bunks, wearing boxers only and sweating like pigs.

I'd hate to think Captain Londry was right, but Bert obviously hadn't a clue in the world I was a cop. I thanked God that I had listened to enough talk radio to know how the wacky Right thought. I could speak the lingo and could suppress the urge to tell him to shut up and cut the shit. I took it slow and purported to have no interest in his exploits at all.

I fed him a line about running guns to Anti-Communists in Mexico. I had meant to say Cuba, but miss spoke. As it turned out, I could have said I was running guns to anti-Communists in Switzerland and it wouldn't have made any difference to Bert. He knew so much about everything, he didn't need to do anything like read or study. We got dinner. It tasted like shit. I was called out of the cell because of an error in my records.

Ed told me they had found Sally's body. She was burned to death in a trailer on the south side of Richmond. The Fire Department suspected arson. We were dealing with Christians of another sort from the Presbyterians back home. He also said, he had slipped something into our food that might make Bert a bit more trusting.

"What in hell is that?" I asked.

"Let me tell you first, it takes one to know one. I have a hunch our boy here likes man meat. I slipped some Viagra in the stew. I figure it will inspire him," Ed said. "I think nothing would inspire confidence more than some cock play."

"What if I ain't inspired?" I asked.

"You got the same dose," Ed said smiling. "Just close your eyes and think of England!"

"I guess I've never passed up a cock before," I said, laughing. He put me back in the cell.

It was even hotter and Bert was looking at me like a cat at a mouse. He knew easy prey when he saw it. Bert was big and downright pretty and I am a scrawny runt. It has always seemed to me when guys are in heat, they don't much care about physical appearance. I looked good to him.

Bert didn't seem to know anyway to get the conversation to sex. I had a thought.

"You're mighty muscular, are you a wrestler?" I asked. "You look like one of the WWF stars."

"No, but I've done some in High School," he said.

"I was a wrestler in High School too," I said.

"You little runt! You couldn't have been a wrestler," he said with the assurance of a guy who didn't have any idea what he was talking about.

"I may be small, but I'm tricky, want to fight me?" I said. "I'll prove it." There was an announcement in the hall, "Lights out in ten minutes!"

"They never turn the lights out in here. They had me on suicide watch," Bert said.

"You ain't going to kill yourself, are you?"

"Shit no!" he said. "They're dumb asses. They're going to erect a monument to me when America sees the light. A fucking monument."

"That's good. I'd hate to be in a bloody cell," I said. Bert laughed. I could see his cock peaking out of his boxers. He was getting excited. The lights went out.

"You're a hairy bastard. You ready to wrestle?" he asked.

"What's the prize for winning?" I asked.

"The usual. I get your ass," Bert whispered.

"We got no lube here," I said

He laughed. "You get to suck it before I fuck ya," he said. He seemed to think this was real clever.

"What if I win? Did you think about that?" I asked.

"I'm a good sport. Turn about is fair play," he said.

"Have you ever lost before?" I asked. He didn't answer right away. I knew what the silence meant. He had more experience than he was willing to admit.

"Shit no, let's wrestle," he said. Bert was a shitty liar.

My playtime with Mark meant I had no problem losing. I could take a cock as well as any guy. What I had glimpsed of Bert's meat assured me he wasn't one of the wonders of the modern world. I planned to win. He was bigger than me, but I was smarter and it was hot as hell. We were sweating like pigs and I was as slippery as a greased pig. The lights went out.

Bert was stupid and knew shit about wrestling. After about 30 seconds I confirmed he had a solid six incher, with some heft. He was dribbling precum and I wasn't too sure he wanted to win. Ed was a smarter guy than I had remembered. He had figured Bert out.

Bert went straight for my boxers and had planned to trip me up with them. I had shucked them the minute the lights went out, so I was naked. He tried to use a few standard holds, but I was too slippery. By then Bert had begun to figure out how big my cock was and he began to fight harder. He wasn't so sure he wanted to be rammed by my donkey dong.

The harder he fought, the more he sweat and the harder it was to get me. The rubbing of our bodies together did nothing to reduce Bert's erection, or mine for the matter. I was horny as hell, the Viagra had taken its effect.

He was big and I was getting tired. Fortunately, Bert finally found my cock and he deep throated it. The match was over. Bert was in love, not with me, but with my dong. Bert was a true cock hound and he had discovered the mother of all cocks. He was worshiping my cock, lapping up the juices flowing from my balls. My balls were oozing like Mt. Vesuvius. This wasn't Bert's first time. The jerk could have gotten a doctorate in cock sucking.

We got in the 69 position and I took a lick. Bert's cock was coated in precum. After the crappy jail dinner, Burt was oozing the food of the gods. I postponed my interrogation and ate desert. I moved my finger to his hole and doubled the flow when I poked it deep in his ass and reached his prostate. I felt sorry this idiot, who could have had a perfectly good life as a cock sucker, had he not fucked it up by following some sicko "born-again" and become a mass murderer.

Bert oozed another massive glob and I lost my train of thought. It's amazing some sex tastes and smells seem to mainline directly to your brain and you can't think. The sucking was real good, but you can't get any information out of a guy when his mouth is filled with your cock. Bert's mouth was overfilled.

"Bert, my cock has an itch I can only scratch with your asshole," I said. "Move and open up."

"You're awfully big," he whined. Bert wasn't a good liar and he didn't sound that worried.

"You're a big boy. You can take it. It may sting some, but you can take it," I said. "You've slobbered me up good. It will fit just fine, it'll slip right in." That wasn't true, at least with anyone I had fucked before, but you can't make an omelet without breaking an egg. Bert was game.

He was already on his back in preparation to being pinned. My cock was dripping with Bert's saliva and my precum. I pivoted and got his legs on my shoulders. I spit on my fingers and worked a few into his ass. He tensed up when I touched his ass hole, but as soon as I forced my way past his sphincter, he relaxed. This was no virgin ass.

I got my cock at his hole and pushed. I took it slow. He was a real muscular guy and if he tensed up too much I figured his muscle bound bubble butt could close me out. I also didn't want to tear him. My cock was the uppermost limit of what Bert could take. He wanted it bad and that helped. It was a slow path deep into his shit tunnel, but I did it and poor Bert was in heaven. My cock filled him completely. Once I was in he clamped tight and it was good for me.

"Do you want this to be fast or slow?" I whispered.

"As slow as you can make it," Bert said. That was fine with me. I calmed down some. He had my cock in a vice-like grip, but with my extra skin, once I relaxed a bit, I could pump my cock shaft while his ass held my skin tight. I was in all the way, but as he relaxed I could still slip in deeper.

"Nice tight ass" I said as I slowly pulsated. These little half inch movements of my cock head seemed to drive him crazy. He was trying to get his hands so he could stroke his cock to climax, but I wouldn't let him. He consoled himself by playing with my tits and chest hair.

"If I'd known jail was this much fun, I'd have blown up something years ago," Bert said. I'm not sure, but I think my cock had found the truth button deep in Bert's rectum. As long as I kept on pressing it, he continued to talk.

"You blew up something?" I asked.

"Sure did. It was in all the papers," he said. "Didn't you see it?"

"Nope. I don't read papers much," I said. "Big thing? Did you get the guys you were after?"

"It was real big, we made a name for ourselves," Bert said. "As I said, they're going to build a monument to us when America comes to its senses." I rubbed the special place and Bert moaned some. "We only got collateral damage. We were trying to get an abortion clinic, but we couldn't park close enough. We only damaged it, but we sure blew the shit out of a Jew Temple."

"You did this by yourself? It sounds like a big job," I said, hoping my big dick in his ass diverted his attention from my poor acting abilities. It did.

"It was a bunch of us guys. We're from Nowheresville and we sure taught some guys a lesson," he continued. "Truthfully, we killed the wrong people. Mostly cops and firemen. I felt bad about that, but Reverend Tommy said, you need to be strong. He and Rev. Paul planned it. I thought Rev. Paul did all of it, but he was working for Rev. Tommy, the Reverend Tommy Carter his self."

"The TV preacher?"

"That's him. You've heard of him?"

"I sure have, big time preacher man."

"He told us we were his army. Too many people were watching him for his people to do the work themselves. He paid for the whole thing," Bert said. "He'll get us good lawyers and get us off. They will get me out of here one way or another." With that comment Bert relaxed and my cock got a little deeper.

"Shit. I'm going to shoot!" I said.

"Fill me up!"

I did. It's embarrassing to say, but I shot one massive load in Bert's ass. This was no dainty spray of cum, I drained my balls and came fucking close to passing out. Tommy Carter, television evangelist and friend of Presidents was at the core of the bombing. It all made sense. How could a little church in an abandoned town, plan and execute such a plot? They were fronts for the big boys and no one was bigger than Reverend Tommy.

I was still draining my balls when Bert asked if he could fuck me.

"I've never done it before," he said.

"I thought you said you always won," I said.

"This isn't strictly speaking true," whispered Bert. "Until I started working for the Army of God, I was kind of a loser. They're the only ones who saw how good I could be. This was my first chance to be famous." I pulled out of his ass, went over to the built in sink and washed off.

Bert was still lying on the floor with his cock hard and pointing straight up. It was dripping with precum. I straddled him, positioned his dick at my ass and sat back. His cock head popped in my ass easily. Bert moaned. I eased back and the entire precum coated shaft slipped in deep. I steadied myself by pinching his pink tits and began doing a little dance on his cock.

It wasn't long before his entire body began to twitch. He shot a good one in my ass. Bert was crying. He said, he had never felt anything so good in his life. I was out of the cell the next morning and I never saw Bert again.

I reported to Captain Londry the results of my night with Bert. He was as excited as I had been and wanted to co-ordinate an expanded investigation. I was discussing this with Londry when word came, Bert was sent to the emergency room. He was dead an hour later. Someone had given him an overdose. Bert was right, they did get him out, one way or the other.

Part 13

I went to see Ed that night. Carter and Chuck were there and we had a good talk. We all had been friends and sex buddies years before, when we were all prison guards. Carter was a big guy, but he had gained more weight and must have been near 300 pounds. His hair and beard were white now. Chuck was still thin and lanky, but he must have been working out. I asked him about that and he said, "Yes", he had been working out. He had a buddy at the gym, a young guy named Sean, who encouraged him.

Ed still had the hang-dog look he had years before. He did look a lot healthier, he had stopped smoking and cut way back on beer. Bert's death was the primary subject of conversation.

"I will swear no one snook anything by me," Ed said. "After that woman was burned, I figured they would go after him. Talk about a real weakest link."

"Who was on before you?" Carter asked in his deep bass voice.

"Washborne and Brown," Ed said.

"Talk about weak link!" Chuck cried. "Brown is a big time Jesus freak. She could have let something by."

"Could it have been someone in the kitchen?" I asked.

"Nope. The trays aren't prepared to any particular room. There would be no way to know who got which tray." Ed said. "I could have been the delivery person. She would have known."

"That was Lizzy, wasn't it?" Carter asked. Ed nodded. "She's okay, her cousin was killed in the bombing. She was hoping for a ticket to the lethal injection. I don't think she wanted him to die too quick."

"I think it's the born again we're after, They are killing the witnesses who could incriminate them. First Sally, now Bert. Someone knew Bert knew way too much and needed to be out of the picture." I said.

"Reverend Johnnie!" Chuck said. "That's who did it."

"Was he around?" Ed asked.

"Who is Reverend Johnnie?" I asked.

"Prison preacher man. He works for one of those prison ministries type organizations," Chuck said. "He makes my skin crawl. He was here the day before visiting prisoners. I'd have never let him in, but Brown might have. She's into salvation."

"Well if it's him, they will catch him soon," I said. "That's about as obvious as could be."

"Not necessarily," Ed said. "Ms Brown has no commitment to the truth. I'd be real surprised if she told them anything about a visit by Reverend Johnnie. The man who runs the jail is a crony of the Mayor. He'll do anything to protect the Mayor and his own ass from looking bad."

"He's got one sad looking ass, there ain't much you can do about that!" Carter said. Everyone laughed. We all had another beer and talked more. It was clear the Preacher was the most likely conduit for the overdose to get into Bert's cell. The doorbell rang. Chuck jumped up and answered it. A minute later he returned with a young man.

"Guys, this is Sean," he said. "You've met Ed before, the big guy is Carter and the small guy is Clydesdale." Sean was maybe 25-27, tall and extraordinarily muscular. He was wearing a tank top which exposed as much of his perfectly smooth skin and beautiful tan as it could. He had a mop of blond hair, straight from the bottle. He wore sweat pants which seemed to be drooping.

He shook hands with me and Carter. It was firm, but not too strong. At least he wasn't trying to impress us with his strength.

"Daddy told me all about you," he said to Carter. Sean turned to me. "And you. He said you were small, but not where it counted!" He winked at me.

"Yea, Clydesdale's got a really big heart!" Ed said. Sean smiled.

"Somehow, it just didn't seem to me Daddy was talking about Clydesdale's heart," Sean said.

"Have a beer," Ed said. "You can join us while we solve the problems of the world." Sean took a beer and sat down with us. We continued talking about Bert's death, but anything that could possibly be a leak vanished from the conversation. Everyone was discreet. It was clear Sean hadn't been following the story. The boy was so in love with Chuck, it was almost comic.

I went off to the bathroom and Chuck was waiting at the door when I got out.

"Clydesdale, I'm sorry, but I told Sean about us when we lived together years ago," he said.

"I hope it didn't bother him" I said. "It was a long time ago."

"It didn't really bother him. It...," Chuck paused, "it turned him on. He'd love to try you out."

"I sure wouldn't mind taking him out for a test drive," I said. "But my dance card is full tonight. I promised Ed."

"I don't think it would bother Sean if we all played," Chuck said. "He says he's never done it in a group, but the idea turns him on."

"We don't play kiddie games. You don't mind seeing another guy's cock in your young friend's ass?" I said. Chuck shook his head and cupped my cock in his hand.

"I seem to have some real distant recollections of some good times in the past," Chuck said. "I sure wouldn't mind a trip down memory lane myself."

"You remember some guys get real hot and bothered when I pop into their ass," I said. Chuck got close to me and whispered.

"Sean's a real nice kid, but he's never completely lost it," Chuck said. "He's always stayed under control. I wouldn't mind if you pushed him as far as you can. He's proud he can hold his feelings in. I'd like to see him loose it. He might need some forgiving after."

We returned to the living room. The beer made everyone convivial and I could tell Sean didn't mind being in a room with older men.

Sean went to the bathroom. When he returned, his baggy sweat pants had slipped and an inch of pubic hair peaked over the drawstring. The conversation was running out and the sexual tension in the room rose. Talk had turned to workout routines and Carter was asking for some advice.

Carter had been unbuttoning his shirt throughout the evening and he now removed it. He must have been working out too. He was real beefy, but well defined and muscular. He was tanned like Sean, but was covered with thick, white fur. Sean all but drooled.

"Let's see your bod," Carter said to Sean. "You ain't shy, are you?" Sean wasn't at all shy. He stripped off his tank top and sweat pants. He was wearing only a pouch type jock. It held his balls and cock only. His pubic hair was above the band. He was shaved smooth except for his pubic region.

"Don't be shy, Sean," Chuck ordered. "These are my best friends, we're all pals. We've all been naked playmates before," Sean stripped off the jock and posed. Carter was naked now and Chuck was stripping. I was thinking about joining in.

Sean was posing and he made sure each pose left his ass hole on view. He had a good cock and nice balls, but I got a clear impression Sean's favorite sex organ was several inches in his ass.

"I don't know about you guys, but I'm tired of pussyfooting around," I said. "Let's all get naked and start fucking."

"Amen, Brother Clydesdale!" Ed cried.

"Now, Brother Chuck, you know we've always been share and share alike guys, but if your friend here is exclusively yours, let us know," Carter asked.

"Shit guys. I've told Sean we all are family and your cock is no different than mine," Chuck said. He looked at Sean. "You'd like to play with my pals?"

"If you would like me too, Daddy?" Sean replied. He was fully erect now and a filament of precum draped from his cock to the floor. The boy was ripe.

"As long as it's in the family, it's fine with me Sean," Chuck said. "Ed, why don't you open him up. I just ask that Clydesdale be the last. I don't want Sean split in half at the start."

"Sean's so pretty, I don't need to shove my donkey dong into that pink hole of his," I said. I never saw a greater look of disappointment on a guy's face as I saw Sean's reaction. He had been watching me as I undressed and had just seen my cock. Sean wanted it badly. "We'll wait and see if Sean is interested and play it by ear," I said. Sean looked relieved. I knew he would be ready when I was.

Ed was right behind Sean and told him to bend over. Ed was no anatomical wonder, but he was nicely hung and about as considerate a fucker as anyone could wish. His dick was slightly wider and shorter than Chuck's and Sean had no problem at all. I was sucking Chuck and felt an odd wave of nostalgia as his cock oozed precum. We had lived together for five years. We were never lovers, but we sure had a lot of fun. I don't think Chuck ever said, No", when I wanted sex play and I know I never turned him down. Carter joined us. His beer can cock was dribbling and Chuck and I alternated sucking it and tasting the sweet goo.

Ed began to moan as he shot a load deep in Sean's ass. Sean was smiling, but hadn't broken into a sweat. Carter was up and ready to replace Ed as Ed's cock pulled from the hole. When I said Carter had a beer can cock, I meant it. It was almost as round as it was long and Sean was stretched. Ed came over to Chuck and me.

"You got a hot one there, Chuck," he said. "You've trained him well."

"Thanks," Chuck said. "I think all those years of practicing with you may have done it." Chuck paused. "It must have been two or three years since I was up your hole."

"Four years and two months to be exact," Ed said. "But who's counting."

"If you wouldn't mind, I wouldn't mind going in again. Lie back and open up," said Chuck. "Are you sure it's been that long?" By then Ed had his legs on Chuck's shoulders and a second later, Chuck's cock vanished deep into Ed's ass. I left them alone and went over to Carter and Sean.

Sean wasn't quite as self assured as he had been with Ed.

"I can prime the pump here, but can't quite get the flow I want," Ed said. Sean was on his knees taking it doggy style. Carter stopped pumping and twitched a few times. I remembered the big man's orgasms. Motionless, but for the twitch. Carter was done, he pulled out and Sean looked at me. I wouldn't say Sean was cocky, but he was self assured, confident he could take whatever came his way.

"Why don't you taste it before you take it?" I suggested. Sean tried to deep throat me, but couldn't get much beyond my head. "Slobber me up good," I said. "Spit is good lube and with all that cum in your ass, I should just slide in." Sean was excited. "Roll over on your back, legs apart and get ready. Sean did what he was told.

Chuck appeared with a tube of lubricant. He coated my cock with it. I toyed with the idea of a single quick thrust, but decided on the slow and easy approach.

"Let me hold your legs open, so Clydesdale can fuck you right," Chuck said. I worked my head into the hole and Sean's tight ass hole peeled back my foreskin. He winced and I pulled out. Chuck added more lube, then I worked it in again.

"Clydesdale used to fuck me. Not real regular, but for special occasions," Chuck explained to Sean. "Too intense for everyday use." I was forcing my cock in, inch by inch. I was half way, at just about the length of Carter's dick.

"It's no problem for me," Sean said. He had a self assured smile on his face. I gave a sudden thrust and impaled him. His eyes glazed over and rolled back into his head. Chuck smiled. Chuck was a sucker and top. He was a reluctant bottom. He knew exactly what Sean was feeling.

Sean looked winded, so I kept on making little pumping movements to keep him that way. He had been half erect when I started, lost his erection when I poked him, but as I pumped, his cock began to re inflate. I began to make deeper thrusts, pulling out four or five inches. His eyes were still glazed, but his cock was rock hard and oozing. Chuck reached over and spread the precum over Sean's cock head.

I pulled all the way out, with my cock head just barely nestled in Sean's hole. Sean seemed to focus. I deep dicked him a few times slowly. On the third or forth time, he began to squeeze his ass.

"Daddy, tell him to fuck me fast, I can't stand this much longer," Sean said to Chuck.

"Sorry Sean. It's his cock. You got to let a guy do what he has to do," Chuck said. "You're his until he shoots." I was in no hurry. It was a good fuck. I pumped him for five or six minutes. Sean was trying to stoke his cock into an orgasm, but Chuck wouldn't let him. He was beginning to moan.

Sean was desperate to shoot, but I varied my thrusting, so he couldn't get used to it. He would build up a head of steam and I would slow down. Ed and Carter joined us and watched the show.

"Damn Clydesdale, your fucker ain't pretty, but it sure is sexy," Ed said. "All man meat."

"All that cum in Sean's ass seems to give your dick a nice sheen," Carter said. "Has your cock always been that veiny, Clydesdale? I've never really watched you fuck before; it's hard to believe its real. It seems to me that vein on the top of your cock is actually throbbing." The longer I fucked him, the more Sean seemed to try to grab my cock with his ass. He was shivering in sexual abandon. Chuck was rock hard. I motioned to him and I pulled out as he shoved his cock in for a home run.

Sean hadn't paid attention, he opened his eyes and found Chuck ramming him. He looked like he had died and gone to heaven. He had been stretched to his limit, now he had the cock of the man he loved deep inside him.

"Is my boy stretched?" Chuck asked. Sean nodded. "Daddy's going to shoot some of his nice man seed in you and make it all better." A few seconds later, Chuck and Sean were climaxing. I still had a full load, but everyone had shot, so I got dressed and went home. I must be getting older. I just got in bed and fell asleep.

The next morning I called Sheriff Earl. We had a lot of talking to do. I was going home for Sally's funeral and I wanted to make sure we got together. Earl wanted me to bring a few of my guys who were completely unknown. He figured the men who burned Sally would likely be at the funeral. All of his men were well known.

I would have loved to take Butch, or Washington, but you could tell they were police, or former military. I settled on Fred, our dumpy accountant and Lonnie, our swishy, former waiter. Fred was one of those guys most people thought they knew. He looked so ordinary, everyone seemed to recall him. Lonnie posed as one of Sally's friends from College. Sally spent three years at Mary Washington College before she decided to get married. No one from town had been there with her at the time, so it was a gap we could explore.

I gave both men the rundown on Sally and Buddy in the car. Fred was always good about remembering. Lonnie was a natural gossip and by the time we reached my Mother's house, you would have sworn Lonnie had been her best friend and confidant in school.

Part 14

Mom was in a state. She was helping Buddy with the kids, doing all the food for the funeral and mad as hell. If Rev. Paul dared to set his foot in the Presbyterian Church, he ran a serious risk of being burned at the stake in the fellowship hall.

Mom also looked ten years younger. She had a purpose in life and a second chance at motherhood. Buddy's children looked on her as their Grandma. My good aunts, Ellen and Becky, were there. Edith was going to come to the funeral. They figured out what Fred and Lonnie were, but looked on them approvingly. Lonnie's experience as a waiter and in restaurant work was a genuine help. After a half hour of knowing Lonnie, Mom decided he would get all the food set in the fellowship hall while she and her sisters went to the service. He changed from being a school friend of Sally's to being a caterer.

Sally's autopsy had been released to the paper the day before. She had been shot before the fire, but wasn't dead. Sally was burned alive. That sent a shiver through everyone's spine. They also found a large tumor in her brain. That explained her behavioral change. Buddy was brow beating himself that he had not taken her to the doctor when she started to act strangely. Becky would have none of that.

"Buddy, you've done everything possible you could have done for Sally and for the kids," Becky said with authority. "You and Clydesdale are the most responsible members of your generation in this family. I won't have any of this kind of talk. Sally is dead and gone. Think about your kids. Pull yourself together and lets get ready for the funeral." I was shocked to find myself listed in the responsible members of the family. Just then the doorbell rang.

I answered it. It was Rabbi Cohen from the Temple in Richmond with Rev. Williams from the Presbyterian Church. Cohen had come to apologize for the thoughts he had. When he found out about the tumor, he realized Sally had been used and had no control over her actions. They spent a half hour with Buddy and the kids and by the time they left everyone felt a lot better. The funeral was good too. Rev. Williams did a sermon which was a masterpiece of reassurance. The television crews were kept at a distance and didn't disrupt the funeral.

I sat in the front of the Church with Mom and Buddy. I sat on the end of the pew so no one could stare at the kids. My Aunts were seated to the rear and keeping track of who was there. They knew everyone and had steel trap memories. Sally was buried in the church yard, right behind the church and we met people in the Fellowship Hall.

Some friends and family came to the house after. Aunt Edith showed up, but kept out of range. She hit it off with Lonnie. Lonnie had that odd, gay hairdresser's way of gossiping with the girls. He chatted away mindlessly and they told him their deepest and darkest. I would need to talk to him later.

I also met Earl's wife. He was out of uniform and casing the place. The second I met her I realized she was lesbian. She was the Gym teacher in High School and needed a husband to be respectable. She was a nice woman. They had worked out a way to deal with the realities of being gay in a small town.

I saw some old friends and relatives, but no one who aroused suspicion. That night, I was in the motel again since Mom's house was filled with relatives. Lonnie and Fred were in the same motel, so we got together at eight in my room. Earl said, he would join us and I had spied Jim, the young kid who knew Ovid and that crew, at the funeral. Earl talked to him. He said, Jim had some more information and would get by after dark.

Fred had been circulating in the crowd at the funeral. He said, most of the people were conventionally shocked and disturbed. He ran into one man, who seemed to think she was a martyr to the cause. Fred only got his first name, fortunately it was an unusual name, Carstairs.

Lonnie said, Edith was disturbed the funeral was at the Presbyterian Church and not at the Victory Temple. Edith also commented, she expected to see more members of the Victory Temple at the funeral. "That woman is totally clueless," Lonnie said. "She didn't seem to understand the relationship between the tumors and Sally's conversion and she didn't believe Sally could have had anything to do with the Bombing. She did make one point. She felt the bombers couldn't have done it, simply because they were too stupid to plan such a thing."

"She might have a point about that," I said.

"Another woman, said much the same thing," Fred said. "Miss Miniver? Or something like that?"

"Miss Minnie Vertue," I said. "She was a sixth grade school teacher."

"She had most of them in her class and had kept up with them," Lonnie said. "She thought they were foolish little boys who let their big dreams get in the way of day to day life. She said, they never carried through with any of their plans. 99% of their schemes never got beyond the big talk stage. She didn't think they were vicious."

"Someone carried a scheme through. There are way to many dead bodies in Central Virginia, that's for sure," Lonnie said. There was a knock at the door. It was Jim. I introduced him to my men. Lonnie perked up at Jim's entrance. There was another knocking at my door. This time it was Earl, the Sheriff and Buck, my old friend from school. Jim was looking real excited. I guessed Slim had told him the Sheriff was a member of the club, but they hadn't been together. Poor Jim was trying to look at Lonnie and Earl without being obvious.

Buck looked at the crowd in my room. He looked disappointed.

"Don't worry," I whispered to him. "They're all members of the fraternity."

"All of them?"

"Tried and tested by me," I said.

"Oh baby," Buck replied. Earl overheard our whispers and smiled. I introduced them to Lonnie and Fred. I caught a glimpse of Jim as he saw Earl and realized he knew Earl.

"This has been a long day. I'm tense as hell," I said. "Anyone up for a rest and relaxation period before we get down to business? I know most of you don't know each other, but take my word for it, you're all real compatible."

"That sounds good to me," Earl said. Lonnie had Jim in his sights and was already naked. Jim was down to his Jockeys in record time. Lonnie was beautiful naked. He looked like a male model. He was toned, tanned, had a hairy chest, but every hair seemed to be in place. I always looked shaggy. He also had a nice cock, pretty, rather than big.

I didn't get to see the cock for long. Jim swallowed it whole.

The next hour was good. It was a mixed group of men with little in common, some of whom didn't know each other. We were a good mix, unified by a common sexual interest. Fred was a dumpy guy with a big cock and that combination hit the spot with Earl and Buck. They quickly formed a triangle on the bed, linked cock to mouth. I joined Lonnie and Jim.

Lonnie was no virgin and I wanted to make sure he didn't push Jim too far. I didn't need to worry. I had guessed Lonnie was a bottom, but knew enough to realize guys aren't often what they look like. I had a tube of lube. Lonnie saw it and smiled. He was now sucking Jim, but he fingered his own ass to let me know of his intentions. Jim was lying back on the bed. Lonnie was on his knees sucking, but he had spread his legs wide so his hole was wide open.

Earl looked over and saw the open invitation. I hoped my new employee didn't mind entertaining a crowd. Lonnie rose and got beside Jim.

"Jim, let me introduce you to Lonnie, my newest employee," I said. Jim giggled.

"It seems we've already met!" Jim said. "He's so handsome." I don't think Jim meant to say that, it just slipped out.

"I don't know if you are much into fucking," I said. "Lonnie is. He likes it in the ass a lot."

"I've never fucked a guy," Jim said. His cock oozed a big bead of precum.

"Hot Damn!" Lonnie said.

"This is your lucky day. Lonnie doesn't mind helping a kid learn about sex," I said, "Do you?"

"Not at all!" my new employee was downright enthusiastic.

"I might do something wrong?" Jim complained. He was worried and excited. He looked around the motel room at all the naked men.

"I don't think there's a snowballs chance in hell you'd do anything I wouldn't like," Lonnie said.

"Everyone here did it for the first time once. We all came back for more," I said. "You're among friends, you have time and no one's going to walk in and spoil the fun." Jim was ready. He got up and Lonnie had his legs on his shoulders. I lubricated Jim's cock and held it at Lonnie's ass.

"Just press and see what happens," I said. Jim was timid. "Push a little harder."

Suddenly, Lonnie's balls were resting on Jim's pubic hair. Both guys looked as if they had just won the lottery. Jim didn't need any more lessons from that point on. Nature took it's course.

"Damn! To be young again," Earl said.

"Thank God, a cock feels just as good in an ass today as it did twenty years ago," Fred said. "Come to think of it, it feels better. I've got no hang-ups to diminish the fun."

"You may be right about that. I've loosened up a lot too. Cocks seem to fit better and go deeper," Earl said. "It's more relaxed. I ain't looking for true love, just a good time, it makes life simpler."

"Boys, I'm normally a top, if any of you are interested, I'd be glad to help you scratch any itch you might have," Fred said. "But I can swing both ways. Clydesdale can tell you, I'm a good sport."

"Looks real filling," Buck said.

"My dick tapers towards the balls," Fred said. "Once it's in, they tell me it's real comfortable." Lonnie was moaning in pleasure as Jim thrust deep. Lonnie must have been the poster boy for the joys of anal sex, bottom position. I was feeling downright inspired. Earl must have read my mind. His cock was poking at my back door. I bent over and let him in.

Earl had a nice average cock and it hit the spot on the first thrust. No stress, no stretching, just cock. Earl was a massager, rather than a thruster. I am a late convert to the bottom and I could recommend Earl as the prefect introduction to that position. He hit all the good spots, just hard enough to make you want more. Thirty seconds later, he would hit the same spot with more vigor and then I wanted him to thrust still harder.

I was thinking of the good times Earl, Slim, Buddy and Buck must have had playing together when I shot off. It caught me completely off guard. Lonnie shot off at the same time. Jim came over and watched Earl pull out of my ass.

"Did it hurt?" he asked.

"Shit no!" I said. "There's enough cum on my chest to use as wallpaper paste. Does it look like it hurt?" I looked at Jim and knew what he was thinking. Earl looked at Jim and we all had the same idea. Buck was twitching on Fred's love pole and had lost it. He was on another planet, alone with Fred and Fred's cock. That was downright inspirational for Jim.

Jim got on the bed beside me and put his legs on the edge, so his hole was open. Earl took some lube and worked it gently into the virgin ass. Jim was rock hard and as Earl worked his fingers deeper, he squirmed.

"Did you ever thing you'd have the Sheriff's cock deep in your ass Jim?" I asked, whispering in his ear. "Is this the first time you've been together?" Jim nodded.

"Just relax," I said. "I know that's hard the first time, but try." Earl leaned forward and whispered to Jim.

"I've got your hole all lubricated and lubricated deep. My cock is dripping and is nestled in you ass. Can you feel where it is?" Earl asked. Jim said, yes.

"Did you feel me press a bit harder and push in a little?" Jim said, yes again. Buck was moaning as he twitched on Fred's cock on the other side of the bed.

"Another little push and my dick will be in you. You're real open. It's not too late to stop. Do you want my cock to be the first in your ass? I understand if you don't. It's a big deal when you open your innards to another man's genitals. It's a cock, oozing ball juice and man seed. Real personal," Earl explained. "Do you want me to push one more time. I'm at the sphincter. Once I'm on the other side of that your ass is mine. Your cherry is popped."

"Fuck me, damn it!"

And fuck Jim he did. I always dread you will fuck a guy for the first time and he will hate it. It is real personal and individual. You never know whether a particular combination of cock and ass will work. Jim and Earl were made for each other. There was a little discomfort when the mushroom pushed through the ass ring, but after that, Jim was fine.

Later we discovered Jim's ass was perfect for Buck's cock and still later, Lonnie's. Jim had discovered a new part of his body and it was thoroughly broken in by ten. We finally got back to business then.

Earl was getting all the telephone records of the bombers and the Victory Temple. He wanted to find a link to outside support.

"The word in school is Ovid knows he's in with a group of homicidal maniacs, and is scared shitless," Jim said. "He would turn State's evidence if he could avoid the death sentence. He's worried about his family."

"Me too," Buck said. "That's my daughter and grandchildren you are talking about!"

"So far they have killed Mr. Edland, Sally and Bert. They tried to get Rev. Williams. And that doesn't include the victims of the bombing in Richmond," I said in review. "Homicidal manic seems likely to me. It seems odd for a act a terrorism to have so many miscellaneous deaths."

"I wonder if we are dealing with two crimes. One an act of political terrorism and another. Maybe a freelancer, who likes to kill people?" Fred said.

"I would guess politically extreme groups might attract people who are extreme in other ways," Earl mused. "The general level of insanity is so high in the group a mass killer, or sadist might just fit in."

I asked, "What if the mastermind is in Greensboro, pulling strings, but one of his puppets is loony. The bad thing is the loony one may be home grown."

"Why do you think that?" Jim asked.

"There was no reason to try to kill Rev. Williams, a small town Presbyterian minister and accidentally kill Mr. Edland. Only someone local knew Williams. I can't believe Rev. Tommy's plan included random murders in a small town."

"Way too many bodies," Earl said. "In my town!" Everyone had to go home for the night, so we broke up. Earl was going to send us video's of the funeral so we could look for suspicious characters. I was bushed and more than ready for bed. There was a knock on the door. It was Lonnie.

"I couldn't sleep. I was thinking," he said as I asked him in.

"About what?" I asked, too tired to be annoyed.

"Your Aunt Edith left the house with the man I talked to earlier, Carstairs," he said. "They were talking in hushed tones and very careful no one was near by. When your mother saw them and ran over to say good bye, they clammed up. I heard your mother asked, if he was Edith's beau. Edith said they had never met, but they had been in a big time huddle, just before your mom saw them."

"That is odd. Edith makes friends slowly, no male friends at all as far as I know," I said. "Thanks for the heads up." Lonnie looked at me.

"I don't know if I can sleep any better," Lonnie said then he paused. "I know you're not my type and I'm not yours, but damn if I don't want your cock in my ass."

"You like big hairy cocks?" I asked.

"Nope. I like thin, smooth boys with matching meat. Jim was almost too macho for me," he confessed. "I just can't stop thinking about that monster of yours pounding the shit out of me."

"Can you take it?"

"I don't know, but I am willing to try."

Lonnie was willing and had no trouble taking it at all. I fucked him like a madman. He loved it that way. By the time he got back to his room, every hair on his body was no longer in place. I hadn't been sure of him before. Lonnie was all right.

Part 15

We brought a video of the funeral back to Richmond. Vince had the Fire Department videos and wanted to see if it was possible to pick out any people who appeared in both. He said that often people as sick as the ones we were dealing with liked to see their victims buried. We didn't have time to compare, but Vince said, he had firemen who had lots of time.

Richmond's Mayor started a moral uplift campaign. He seemed to think the bombing was God's judgment on the sinfulness of modern life. He started to hold rallies. These were poorly attended, but were good for our investigation. We found out who the Mayor's friends and associates were.

The Fire and Police Departments took the campaign really badly. The bombing had killed more of their members than any other event in Richmond's history and they didn't like the idea their dead were sinners at all. A television reporter asked the Mayor that question point blank.

"Are you saying, Sir, the men and women killed in the bombing were sinners?" she asked.

"No, they paid for the sins of others," the Mayor said with a smug assurance.

"You mean God kills the innocent to punish the guilty?" she asked.

"Things like abortion, homosexuality and....," the Mayor got lost in his reply.

"Being Jewish, Mr. Mayor?" the reporter filled in the blank. The Mayor was in shit up to his eyeballs by then and left the room. That interchange got on national news. I thought he would keep his mouth shut after that, but no such luck. He got to be a celebrity on some of the stranger talk shows and his campaign was well financed by some deep pocketed extremist.

Captain Walker, the man in charge of the investigation for the city and the bookkeeper in charge of the Fire Department weren't powerhouses of drive and intelligence. They weren't bad men, just the wrong men.

I was shocked when Wilmot Evans, the Fire Chief-Accountant appeared at my office.

"Mr. Noland, I would like to speak with you about the Temple Bombing," he said in his somewhat prissy, very precise way. "We have a theory about the event and I understand you have an alternative view. We have been working under the assumption it is the work of foreign terrorists, probably Arab and probably Anti-Semitic."

I explained my theory. It was the work of home-grown terrorists, primarily anti-abortion, but with a strong ultra right wing aspect. "I wouldn't be surprised if Anti-Semitism and anti Gay elements aren't part of the brew, but I think it's mostly born-again and holier-than-thou." I outlined my evidence, not telling him some important parts of the story.

"Well, Mr. Noland, I would outline the case for foreign terrorists for you, but as you well know, there is no such case," Wilmot said. "Captain Walker at the Police Department and I went through all the files this weekend. I am an accountant. Nothing added up. The foreign terrorists do not exist, their plot does not exist. We have been chasing a mirage."

"That's the way I see it," I said.

"The Mayor and I are very close, did you know his wife is my niece?" I shook my head. "I can not endanger the Department, my men and the people of the city with this charade. Captain Walker feels the same way. We must redirect the investigation."

"Actually, Mr. Evens, we would kind of like it if you, officially at least, leave it as it is. We think the bombers have been lulled into a false sense of security. If you can keep the Mayor off our backs, that would be help enough."

"I can see your point," he said. "We can share information."

"We already are, Sir," I said. "We are well coordinated with both the Fire and Police Department."

"That explains it," Wilmot said. "When Walker and I went over the files, we realized the official theory wouldn't hold water. We wondered why we hadn't had rebellion in the ranks. They were already working on your theory."

"Yes, Sir."

"That makes me feel better," he said. "You have our support. Is the Mayor involved?"

"Up to his eyeballs, I'm afraid."

"Sandra, my niece and her mother fear that too," Wilmot said. "Sandra feels there is something dreadfully wrong. Her husband has changed. She thinks he thought he made a deal with a prophet and made it with the devil instead. I don't think he can be saved politically."

"Captain Walker and I want to save our Departments," he continued. "After the loss of personnel following the Mayor's election, the disaster of the bombing and this botched investigation, I need to save the Department's reputation." With this declaration he left.

I called Vince and told him about the conversation.

"Do you think he was trying to get information for the Mayor? Could he be a mole?" Vince asked.

"I don't think so," I said. "I think he was genuinely shocked at the investigation. He's a bean counter who was put in an impossible situation. My guess is, he has more guts than the Mayor thought. The Mayor thought he had a rubber stamp and Wilmot Evans has some backbone."

"We will know soon enough," Vince said as he hung up. The phone rang immediately; it was Ed.

"Do you remember my mentioning Reverend Johnny?" he asked.

"Sure."

"Well he likes to do some of his saving at the Southern Bar and Grill on Jefferson Davis Highway," Ed said. "It's a motorcycle, drug drop kind of place. Word came back the good Reverend has been in a particularly exalted mood since Bert died. You might check it out. It's Friday, they'll have a good crowd there."

"Have you been there?"

"I sure have, but they know I'm a prison guard. They clam up," Ed said. "With your good looks and commanding presence, you should fit in great. There will be a full crew tonight." I thanked him for the info. Lonnie came in the room.

"Do you know anything about the Southern Bar and Grill?" I asked.

"Not my kind of place. Drunks, bikers and fags, heavy into leather," he said.

"Would I fit in?"

"You sure as hell would," he said. "They like guys big there, 250 plus, but your big where it counts. I'd wear something to advertise your meat and you'll be beating them off with a stick." That evening I went to the restaurant and took a seat at the bar. I was wearing an old flannel shirt and older jeans.

I was unbuttoned to my navel and had not brushed my hair or beard, so I looked a bit like a wild man.

I asked for a Bud and nursed it while watching a NASCAR race on the television. No smoking regulations don't apply to Jefferson Davis Highway. Everyone there was a regular, so I stood out, especially since I had showered in the last day or so, and didn't share the stale smell of beer and cigarettes that filled the room.

"What brings you here, Mister?"

"Bad luck," I said. "I was supposed to have a hot date with a girl in Colonial Heights and the bitch stood me up."

"Have another beer," the guy said. "Beer is a lot more dependable than a bitch, any day. I'm Skeeter." Skeeter was about 200 pounds, with dirty blond hair and a beard. I guessed he was 35 or so.

"Beer is good, but you can't fuck it," I said. "They call me Donkey Man." Skeeter took a glance at my crotch.

"Now how did you get a name like that?"

"I kicked my Momma so much before I was born, they thought she was going to give birth to a donkey," I said. "They didn't know I was going to be a hairy bastard until I got older." Skeeter laughed. Every time I turned to look at the NASCAR race, he stared at my crotch. He introduced me to a guy named Beau and another guy named Buddy. Beau was deeply tanned, with curly black hair and a barrel chest. I looked at his hands and knew he was a carpenter. Buddy was tall and thin and was an auto mechanic.

They all sympathized with my woman problems. They liked my Donkey Man story and each looked at my crotch as I told it. They all knew the real story. All were interested.

"Most girls wouldn't recognize a real man if she found him. They want to go dancing and partying. You can't do that every night when you're working construction," Beau complained. "I leave at five to get to work, I can't stay up to one or two in the morning."

"I know what you mean," Buddy said. " They say, "Your hands are too dirty". Shit, I'm a mechanic. You can't fix a car without getting dirty!"

"I'll bet they get real lovey-dovey, when their car breaks down," I said.

"You're real perceptive, Donkey Man. They'll call, "Buddy I'd love to see you, can you come over. And bring your tools " I'll go over knowing I'll fix the car, but probably she'll let me fuck her for payment. The last time that happened, her God Damned mother showed up." Everyone laughed.

"Do not use the Lord's name in vain!" a high shrill voice screeched.

"It's the fucking Preacher!" Beau said.

"Preacher man! Come over here," Skeeter called. "Donkey Man here needs for you to pray for him, so he can get laid tonight!" Rev. Johnny was thin, pasty, pale, clean shaven and had small features. He clearly rarely saw the light of day. He had a spectacularly coiffed hair do, a combination of Elvis and TV evangelist. Every hair was sprayed in place. He came over to see us.

"You laugh at me, but you will pay someday," he said. "Fire, brimstone and death shall be on your heads. God punishes. I am his prophet and his hand."

"If that's the way you feel about it, don't pray for me to get laid," I said. "Personally, I think I might do better on my own." My companions were dazzled at my witty repartee. "I'm Presbyterian, either I was destined to get laid or not. It was all decided before time began." One of my Aunts had used a variant of the line to shut up a troublesome neighbor, who thought it was awful she drank wine with dinner. Reverend Johnny looked puzzled, said, "Humph!" and left us. My new friends burst into gales of laughter.

"You need come to here regular," Buddy said. "We've never gotten rid of him so quickly before."

"He's a pest?" I asked.

"Harmless," Skeeter said.

"I'm not so sure about that," Beau said. "Remember last week? When he said, he didn't need a gun? That was strange."

"What did he do?" I asked. "I'm no giant, but I could sure handle him."

"He was saying he would get us. I said, are you getting a gun? And he said, he didn't need a gun. He could do us in and nobody would be the wiser," Beau explained. "I thought that was just his typical line of bullshit, but then he added, "like Burt", or Robert or some name like that."

"I asked. "Who in hell is Bert?" and he clammed up and left," Skeeter added. "It was strange."

"He looks like a strange one to me. I'd keep away from him," I said. They told me more about him. He was Rev. Johnny Millbank and he had a store front church on Hull Street. It was called the 'Open Bars Ministry'.

"He likes prisoners and drunks a lot," Beau said. "We drink, but we aren't drunks. Not anymore."

"He wants to save them?" I asked.

"I think he really wants to feel superior to them," Beau said. "Tommy over there in the corner got in trouble once and the Reverend didn't do shit."

"The way we're putting down beers, I'm going to be in trouble soon," I said. I was feeling good by then.

"Don't you worry one bit about that. I live in the trailer park right behind here," Beau took a long look at my crotch and the outline of my cock in my pants leg. "Many a guy has slept it off in my double wide." He looked me in the eye. "They had a damn good time too."

I knew exactly what he was hoping for.

"Beau's a real friendly guy. He's helped us all out from time to time," Skeeter said.

"I hope you guys help him out too," I said. There was a pause in the conversation.

"We sure do," Buddy said. "Guys can be real helpful. If they're open minded."

"No one is more open minded than me," I said. My cock was beginning to react to the talk and they all noticed that.

"Another round of beers for my friends here," I said. It wasn't eight yet and I was a bit afraid we would be too drunk by the end of the night to have any real fun. The room was real smoky, but I began to get a whiff of non cigarette smoke. I looked toward the kitchen and saw smoke billowing from the kitchen.

"I just got a call. The cops will be here in ten minutes. They got sniffer dogs with them. It's time to leave," I announced in my best bull-horn like voice. There was dead silence and everyone began to move. Several dead drunks managed to get up and out. Thirty seconds later, the place was empty.

"What in hell was that about?" Beau asked. The bartender looked pissed.

"The place is on fire. Let's get out of here," I said. The bartender looked back at the kitchen. "Oh shit!" he said as he dialed 911.

It was cool and nice outside. Skeeter had to go to see his parents in Emporia, leaving me with Beau and Buddy. "How close is your trailer?" I asked. Beau looked at me and smiled. There was a 7-11 next door, so I picked up two six packs and we all adjourned to Beau's double wide. We could hear the fire engines in the distance.

Beau's trailer wasn't what I expected. It was clean and neat with pictures of three children everywhere.

"Bad divorce?" I asked when I saw them.

"That would be the nice way to say it," Beau said, bitterly. "Get in the shower Buddy! You know the routine." Buddy left the room for the bath. "It's one thing to get dirty at work, another to leave the dirt at home. I need to shower too, do you mind?" Beau asked.

"Not at all. I wouldn't mind a little freshening up myself," I said.

"Jump in the shower with me!" Beau said.

"Is Buddy with the program?" I asked.

"Big time," Beau said. "He's the one who gave me some lessons."

It turned out neither man was a virgin. Beau was somewhat new to it and a bit reserved. Buddy was a wild man, open to anything and everything.

Beau was hairy with a nice compact set of balls and dick. He was cut and had a solid, six-inch, tube of man meat. Buddy was thin, with hair on his chest and a trail to his pubic forest. He was uncut with six or seven inches of not too thick cock. Beau was quiet and didn't show much emotion. He leaked non stop, so you knew under his calm exterior his juices were churning. Beau was one of those guys who stares at your cock and seemed to be unsure if he will touch it, then swallows it whole and won't stop sucking until he has drawn every drop of cum from your cock.

Buddy was the opposite. He was enthusiastic about everything, wide open to my cock and not shy one bit about what my cock felt like as I rammed him. Beau had told me to fuck him good, while we were in the shower. "It's the only way you can calm him down," he said.

Buddy was ready. He admitted my cock was a size or two bigger than he was accustomed to, but he was ready. We tried it spread eagle style first, but it hurt too much, so he decided to sit on it. It was good for me, but strange for Buddy. Buddy didn't enjoy my cock; he craved it. I think he must have been one of those guys who take being a size queen really seriously. Everyone likes to look at big cocks, but not all want them rammed in their ass.

Buddy wanted it in his ass, all the way, to the hilt. He was willing to work for it and he didn't care what he had to do to get it in. I really don't like hurting guys, least of all in the ass. You think of the apparatus as being utilitarian, but it's all really delicate. I've spent enough time in an ass to know the intense feeling you get when your cock and cock head touch the membranes and organs in a guy's ass, don't come from rubbing against calluses. It's all tender inside the hole. The cock is the organ of touch.

Fortunately, the tight hole that was a problem for Buddy felt great to me. Buddy was a hot fuck. Beau was turned on by watching his friend take my dick. Buddy finally got used to it and got to spend some quality time in places he had never been before.

I spent some time in those places when Mark fucked me and I sent my friend John there many times. I was a little afraid Buddy would be uncomfortable taking the trip in front of Beau, his friend. Beau helped Buddy along. Beau never lost his erection the whole time we were fucking. I realized, Beau liked to watch and we sure put on a good show.

If Beau wanted a demonstration of every way you can force a cock into an ass, Buddy and I did it. Buddy got loosened up after the first half hour, either that, or his ass hole was so tired he couldn't resist anymore. Beau is a man of few words, those words being, "look at that fucker slide in that hole," and "fucking hot!"

His cock was hard and dripping the whole time, I leaned over and licked the precum several times. Both Beau and Buddy liked that. Buddy finally came and fell asleep immediately. Beau looked relieved. He was lying on the bed, so I straddled him and sat on his cock.

I totally surprised him.

"Shit, I haven't been in a hole since my wife left me," he said. I began grinding my ass on his love pole.

"Just think of it as a man cunt," I said. He was enjoying it a lot.

"You're tighter than that bitch ever was," he said. I figured out what would really make his day.

"How did you like to fuck her? Doggy style?"

"On her back," he said.

"Let's do it that way then," I said.

"I cum real fast that way."

"Shove it in and let nature take it's course." That's what we did. Beau was right, he popped quickly, but it was the right angle for his cock and my prostate, so it worked out well for both of us. Beau was a happy camper.

Part 16

Buddy had to get to work early, so he was out of the trailer at six. I took a second ride on Beau's cock and then went to work. I made a call to the Richmond police as soon as I got back.

The Richmond Police arrested Reverend Johnny before noon. They searched his house and found a bottle of the drug Bert overdosed on. My connection in the police, Bob Miller, told me Johnny was all but bragging about it when a real high powered lawyer showed up and made him shut up. The drug came from a pharmacy in Charlotte, North Carolina and was made out to a man named Carstairs McMillian. I relayed the comment from the funeral about a man named Carstairs.

Bob Miller had been a second from the bottom detective when I had been on the force. He had risen to the top due to the shake up in the Department. He was more dogged than bright I thought, but he had been working with us from the start. He wanted to find the bombers as much as we did. I was surprised at how fast the investigation progressed with the new information. Bob wanted to prove he deserved his new rank in the department. He just needed a break to make an advance. That was fine with me.

Miller was onto the North Carolina connection like a hound on a fox. When it came to basic everyday police work, Bob was good. I sent Lonnie to the Southern Bar and Grill to see what the reaction there was to Johnny's arrest. I wondered if he had been bragging to other patrons of the bar about his exploits.

Lonnie called me a 8:00 that evening with his cell phone. A guy had been there asking about Beau and his friends. No one knew where they were and the man had left his phone number and a promise of a hundred dollars for anyone who called. Lonnie followed the man out and saw his car had North Carolina plates. I was on my way to Beau's trailer in ten minutes.

Beau hadn't gone to the bar yet. I told him the whole story and said, he was going to be bunking with me for a while. We called Skeeter and Buddy and told them to lay low and keep away from the Southern Bar and Grill. No one knew much about them, including where they lived and worked. Beau thought no one would tell the guy where he lived since everyone disliked the Reverend so much. I reminded him the nights were long and boozy. A hundred dollars might look good at two in the morning.

I was afraid Beau would be pissed I had used his information to get the Reverend. Fortunately, he was really interested. He had been shocked at the bombing and had done some volunteer work in the aftermath. He had found a body in the apartment house for the elderly and took it real personally. Beau was more than willing to help. He packed fast, grabbed his photographs of his kids and we left. It was a furnished trailer and he had no possessions at all.

Beau was also looking for a new job, having just finished framing a house the week before. When I got to my office, I called John and asked if he needed some new guys working for the Millennium Construction Company. John said, he'd talk to Beau tomorrow. Lonnie already had called in his information to Bob Miller. By the time we got back to the office, the police had followed the clues. The phone number was for a motel room. The car was not registered. The license plate was a fake, no such number existed in the North Carolina DMV. A few minutes later Vince dropped by.

He was in his Fire Department Chief's dress uniform and looked mighty impressive. I introduced him to Beau. They both liked what they saw. Vince had been at a promotion ceremony and had talked to Wilmot Evans.

"I think I misjudged the man," Vince said, "He is sure on board now. Big advances on all fronts." I told him of my talks with Bob Miller.

"Bob is like a lazy Basset Hound who gets a scent," I said. "He's on the trail and won't let go until he has tracked down the killers. They must know the noose is tightening." I told Vince about Beau's role in unraveling the plot.

"It's private citizens like you who have driven this investigation," Vince said.

"I helped by accident," Beau said, "Donkey Man made the connections."

"Donkey Man?" Vince asked. I explained my deception. Vince had a good laugh at that.

"If you like Donkey dicks, or horse cocks, or Tonsil Ticklers, Vince here is the man for you," I said. "He has the meat to beat."

"Are you guys members of a club?" Beau was smiling as he asked this, but I knew he was interested and wanted to know more about Vince.

"Not exactly a club," I said, "although they are building one. I guess it would be best to say, we are a group of like minded guys."

Vince looked Beau in the eye. "I take it you are a like minded guy too?"

"I don't really know," Beau said. "I like to suck cock and get sucked. Does that make me one of the guys?" Vince let out a belly laugh.

"It sure goes a long way!" he said, still laughing. "Something about the way you said that makes me think this might be the first time you've admitted that. Beau, you're among friends, here. We're all cock suckers. We're all men who like man sex."

"Why don't you guys get comfortable upstairs," I suggested. "I'll join you shortly." They went up and I sat down looking at messages from earlier in the day. By the time I went upstairs, Vince and Beau were naked and sucking.

Vince was usually 100% top. He too discovered Beau's warm spot for fucking. Beau was such a nice guy, you wanted to help him out. I had helped him out the night before, Vince helped him tonight. It was about ten and for some reason I wanted to fuck. Usually a nice J.O. session will meet my needs, but I really wanted to fuck. I realized we were without a real bottom in my bedroom. I got up, dressed and went downstairs to the office. Everyone was busy there, so I wandered over to John's house. It was dark. A car drove up. The window rolled down.

"Hey there, short, hairy and ugly. Looking for a good time?" I was going to say something nasty when I recognized the voice. It was Tom, one of John's superintendents.

"What are you doing out this late?" I asked.

"We had a bad pour for a floor slab, we spent the last six hours trying to fix it. I had to drop the company truck off at the back," Tom said. "I have to drive home, then get back here at six tomorrow."

"You can spend the night here, if you don't mind the commotion," I said. I got up to the window. "I am in the mood for some hot and heavy fucking tonight. Are you game? It's a great relaxer."

"I'm really tired," Tom said that in a way that indicated he could be convinced really easily.

"When was the last time you shot off?" I asked. That comment was enough to change his mind. I had never fucked Tom before, but I knew he liked the bottom. We had partied together and he has seen me in action, so he knew what he was getting into.

"Do you think you could fuck me to sleep?" he asked. I said, we could sure try. We went back to my apartment.

Vince was sitting on Beau's cock when we got to the bedroom. Tom was a regular at John's house and was a participant in the open sex there, so he just stripped and took a shower. Vince had to go home, so he dressed and left. Beau took a shower to clean up after his fuck session with Vince. The two men joined me in my bedroom.

Tom is short, muscular, with dirty blond hair. He was good looking and Beau, who looked a bit like Bluto, was obviously taken with him. I thought I might have lost my chance for a fuck for the night.

"There's no way the donkey dick can fit in your ass," Beau said. "That fucker must weigh more than you do."

"Seeing is believing," Tom said. I had planned to have a nice utility fuck. Quick in, quick out and no bother. Tom was thinking the same way, but neither of us had considered our cocks and their feelings.

It didn't turn out the way I expected. I was sitting on the edge of the bed and Beau took a hankering to my cock. We had sucked the night before, but Beau seemed to have relaxed some and was doing a first rate job. Beau had his ass in the air and open. Tom was inspired by this and fingered Beau's ass. I was going to tell Tom, Beau was a top, but I figured Beau was an adult and could take care of himself.

Tom decided to lubricate Beau's ass with spit, using his tongue as an applicator. Beau seemed to like this a lot. All this attention to Beau's ass turned Beau into a first rate sucker. His interest in my cock seemed to increase with Tom's interest in his ass. We all knew exactly where this was heading.

Beau was trying to swallow my entire cock. I pivoted so we could 69. I was at Beau's cock. He had spread his legs, so Tom could rim him. Tom was inches from my face as I sucked Beau's dribbling cock. Tom sat back and a few seconds later, his cock appeared, hard as a rock and aimed at Beau's virgin ass hole. He poked his mushroom in the hole a few times. Beau moaned. He pulled out, coated his cock in spit, then shoved it deep.

As Tom's cock vanished in Beau's hole, my cock vanished in Beau's throat. He deep throated me, for only the second time in my life. I started to shoot,

Beau shot and Tom popped at the same time. It was good. We broke apart and I fell asleep. Orgasms are the best sleeping pills.

Next morning I took Beau over to John's office to see if Beau could get a job. Skeeter, John's tenant was there. Skeeter did most of the hiring of labor. It was clear John had clued him in on Beau's situation. They hit it off well and Skeeter hired him on the spot and offered him a bed in the attic until the murderer was caught.

I felt like I had done my good deed for the day, but when I got back to my office there was a call from Buddy, the mechanic and the Sheriff from home. I called Buddy first. He said, a guy had been by looking for him, but the girl at the counter had told the guy it was his day off. I told him to get over to my office right away and have the girl call Miller. I also told Buddy to check his pickup before he drove it.

I called the Sheriff next. He said, Slim was worried. There was lots of activity at the Victory temple and something was afoot. He was trying to get a search warrant, but the Judge was balking. He was a Baptist and a big time born again. He said, he was afraid of church versus state issues. Sheriff Earl had other ideas. About a minute after we hung up, my Mom called.

"Your Aunt's acting strangely," she said. "Edith's always acted strangely, but she called and said good by, she was going on a trip."

"She ain't the cruising type, is she?"

"She had that pompous, exalted air she has when she's thinking about God and getting ready to do something stupid," Mom said.

"Like when she gave all that money to the missionary?"

"Like that, but much worse. Muttering stuff like, she's sorry for all the things she's done, but she never meant any harm," Mom said.

"Call the Sheriff, now!" I said. "He thinks something is afoot, he needs to know."

"Do you think it's that serious?"

"I sure as shit do!" I had forgotten I was talking to Mom. She was so concerned, she forgot to complain about my language. She said, she'd call now.

At noon, Earl raided the Victory Temple. The place had twenty or so "True Believers" praying inside. Earl took them out for questioning and they had just cleared the sanctuary when the building burst into flame. Lots of minor injuries, glass cuts and bruises caused by flying debris, no fatalities among the "True Believers", or the police. Earl told me about it from his cruiser radio.

"Watch out for a second bomb!" I screamed at him.

"Shit, you're right!" he exclaimed as he hung up. The Fire Department had just arrived. I later found out they stayed back and the second bomb exploded, with only minor injuries. It had been a canister of shrapnel. It was a man killer.

By now Buddy was at my office. I got Lonnie to find Skeeter and reel him in. The bad guys were in a killing frenzy. They had lost, but they might try to do a lot of damage before they were caught.

I turned on the news. Much to my surprise, the Richmond Police had road blocks throughout the city, checking for bombs and suspects. The Police and the Fire Department Arson investigators had arrived at the Mayor's house that morning and they gave up all pretense of following the Mayor's instructions. I thought they had heard of the new bombing at the Victory Temple.

Wilmot Evans called and told me they had a search warrant for the Mayor's house and office and were going thought it with a fine tooth comb.

"How is your niece? I asked.

"She and the kids are at my house. She found something on his computer last night. Her thirteen year old removed the hard disk and brought it in. It's very bad," he said. "Very bad."

"Do you have a Police guard at your house?" I asked. There was silence.

"There will be," he said, as he hung up the phone.

My Mom called later in the day. She and Aunts Ellen and Becky were off to post bail for Edith.

"She has a bad cut, so they are letting her go. No one's telling anything," Mom said. In the background I could hear Aunt Becky ranting. "There are no Miranda rules in this house. If we're posting bail, that foolish girl will tell us everything!" Mom said she was off and then she asked if I could come home to help out. "We feel a bit exposed here."

I said, sure.

A huge Winnebago drove up to my office. My first thought was another bomb, but Lonnie waved to me from the passenger side window. Skeeter lived in the motor home, so they drove it over. I told Butch I need to go to Mom's. He understood. The Police were doing their jobs, so I wasn't needed. Skeeter offered to give me a ride. The motor home was fully outfitted with phones, a satellite dish, a computer and a television. I agreed. Buddy, the mechanic joined us, so Skeeter, Lonnie, Buddy and I took off.

Lonnie had been a truck driver at sometime in his career, so he drove and I watched the Television and made calls from the living area. The Charlotte police had closed in on the North Carolina part of the operation. The scheme had unraveled. I could relax.

The trip was four hours in my car, in the Winnebago, it was five and a half. We had some time to kill. I was thinking of taking a nap. Buddy and Skeeter had another plan.

"Buddy here tells me you got the Dick of Death," Skeeter commented. "Do you give rides?"

"I've been known to give a guy a trial run, if he's into it," I said. Skeeter looked at me long and hard. He swallowed.

"I'm into it," he said, almost whispering. I caught the look on Buddy's face. I realized Buddy didn't know Skeeter bottomed. Skeeter was a big, blond, redneck. I knew how difficult it was for him to admit he wanted it in the ass. I smiled at him.

"That sounds good to me. Do you want to take a look at my fucker before you get on board?" I asked.

"I'd sure like that," Skeeter replied. He looked at me closely again. "I'd like a real close look."

"Hey, Lonnie!" I yelled. "Avoid potholes for the next few miles. We're getting up close and personal back here and I don't want to hurt anyone." I stripped naked. Buddy was already nude and Skeeter stripped slowly. He was uneasy. He wanted my cock bad, but he was obviously embarrassed. Buddy knew why. Skeeter was on the floor looking at my cock while I sat on a bed. Buddy joined him.

"You've been holding out on me. How often do you take it in the ass?" Buddy asked. He was speaking softly. "Donkey Man's cock was in my ass for a good hour and a half last night. I never got to look at it close like now. Look at that beautiful bead of man juice on the slit! Do you want it? I'll take it if you don't." They stuck out their tongues together and shared it. "You were such a good top, Skeeter, I never guessed."

"I've done it once or twice," Skeeter said.

"You liked it, didn't you?"

"Yep."

"You liked it a lot more than you were willing to admit. Didn't you?" Buddy asked. Skeeter tried to swallow my cock whole in response.

"Donkey Man's cock is different from the usual fuck," Buddy continued. "It fills up every space you have left over in your innards. I felt he was reaching toward my heart. Like his was giving me CPR in my ass. You're going to love it."

Part 17

Skeeter was timid and tight, but he wanted my cock so bad he was willing to put up with a lot. I was willing to help him out. It wasn't easy getting in, but his interest never flagged. Buddy was a first rate bottom, so he coached him. He also gave Skeeter a few snorts of Rush. Once I got fully embedded and the poppers took effect, all was well.

Deep in his heart Skeeter was a strong, silent type, red neck. My cock pushed him over the edge and he was a moaning and whimpering mass of male hormones. He was on that razor thin edge between ecstasy and pain. My horse cock was the absolute limit as to what he could take. He was like a violin and my cock was the bow. Every movement of my cock made him moan, twitch, or shiver.

My dick was a true joy stick and small movements caused convulsive reactions in Skeeter. I had started thinking his would be a nice utility fuck to get my rocks off, but I got into it kind of deep. He was real tight and I didn't think I could pile driver fuck him without hurting him. It was one of the few times when I felt every square inch of my cock had bonded to his ass. Every nerve in my fuck tool was sending pleasurable signals to my brain. I knew my cock in his ass was in total control of his emotions.

I would pull out and his ass would try to hold my cock head in a vice-like grip. As I pushed in, he reacted to every movement and by the time I was deep in him, he could hardly breathe. Before Skeeter, I had thought of the ass as a hole. Skeeter's ass had lips that caressed my cock and after some effort, opened to let me into his love tunnel. I will swear his ass kissed my cock.

My balls were telling me to pound the shit out of the guy and shoot. My mind told me to be careful and take my time. Lonnie pulled off the road to see what was going on in the back. I was getting into the same state Skeeter was in. Every sexual nerve was raw, but I couldn't pop.

Lonnie saw my predicament and came to my rescue. He stripped, lubricated his cock and popped it into my back door. The second his cock head hit my prostate, I popped and that was enough to send Skeeter over the edge. Buddy lunged forward when he saw the first glob of cum emerge from Skeeter's cock. He swallowed every drop.

When I finally pulled out, I felt as if I was a pound or two lighter. There wasn't a single drop of cum left in my body. Skeeter looked as happy as any man could be. I felt pretty good too. Lonnie had popped in my ass, got dressed and went back to driving.

"Damn, that was hot!" Buddy said. "Skeeter, my buddy, I forgive you for holding out on me about bottoming. That was the best show I've ever seen. Damn. I didn't know you had it in you."

"I didn't either," Skeeter said. "Shit. I'm sorry. I lost it."

"Hey, we're pals," Buddy said. "How many times have you cracked my nut? Thirty, forty times? It seems to me you've dropped a load in my ass every time we've had a chance too."

"I guess so," Skeeter replied.

"Have I ever pretended to not like being fucked? Shit no,"Buddy said.

"It was embarrassing," Skeeter said.

"Why, because you enjoyed yourself? Because you shot the biggest load of your life?" Buddy continued. "You never complained when I hit the back wall of the trailer with my jiz. Did you? You finally relax enough to let it all hangout and you're embarrassed? Come on!" To emphasize the point, Buddy leaned over and lapped up some of his friends cum as it quivered on the blonde's still oozing cock. He licked it up.

The rest of the trip was uneventful until we got to Mom's. When we got to my house, I went in alone. Aunts Becky and Ellen were being nice to Edith. Edith's condition was not good. The cuts from the explosion had required 67 stitches so she was in shock. She looked like shit. The combination of the cuts and the embarrassment of being used by the Preacher had taken a toll on her. My Aunts took mercy on her.

Mom and Ellen led her to bed. Becky filled me in on the local news. The Preacher had vanished, leaving the flock to fend for themselves. It was finally dawning on the "True Believers", the Preacher planned to burn them up in the Temple and he apparently was not planning to take the trip to heaven with them.

There was an all points bulletin out for the Preacher, but his car was left at the Temple. He must have been using another car no one knew about. The town was an armed camp, with the local Police and State Troopers very much in evidence. There were a lot of hunting rifles ready for use too. The full extent of the Temple's activities were now known and most realized there was a mass murderer on the loose.

My cousin Buddy came by with his two children. Becky was going to take them to her cottage on the Outer Banks for a week. Buddy felt it would be a good idea to get them away from town until the Preacher was captured. He assumed the Preacher was the killer. I didn't mention there probably was another murderer. It was possible the mass murderer was the Preacher, but I doubted that. Someone had killed Mr. Edland and Buddy's wife and who knows how many other people by now. He was at large too. I guessed the Preacher wasn't the sort who got his hands dirty, let alone covered in blood.

There was so much excitement in town the kids wanted to stay, but Becky was obviously a favorite aunt and a fun woman to boot. They went off with her without too much complaint.

Ellen returned from putting Aunt Edith to bed. She and Mom were going to stay with Edith 24/7, until Edith was feeling better and had told them all they wanted to know.

"She is a foolish woman and the only way she can redeem herself is to tell all," Ellen said. "I know she knows more than she admits. If she will babble in her sleep, I will be taking notes!" I told her I had some men to stay at the house and protect them if necessary. She said it wasn't necessary, they could take care of themselves. She did not insist, so I realized she was relieved to have a man around. Lonnie appeared. They had been at Sally's funeral with him and seemed to think of Lonnie as an old friend.

I took Buddy to the Winnebago and introduced him to the guys. When Buddy, my cousin, met Buddy the mechanic, they clicked immediately. I had never seen love at first sight, but it was damn close. Cousin Buddy offered to take Buddy, the mechanic, to his house, so it would be less crowded. It would be more restful, he said. I doubted rest was on their minds.

Sheriff Earl and Slim drove up. They were checking on Edith.

"You know there was no real justification for letting Edith off," Earl said. "It's just that she was so pathetic. I was hoping to question her."

"No chance of that now, she's sleeping," I said, then I told him of Ellen and Mom's plans. He chuckled.

"They may have a better chance of getting something out of her than me," he said. "Are they serious about questioning her?"

"Dead serious. Mom has tendencies to be merciful, Ellen can't tolerate fools, least of all in the family," I answered. "Ellen was a legal secretary. She knows the ropes and takes diction at a million words a minute. Don't worry, if Edith says anything they will get it word for word."

I introduced Earl and Slim to Buddy and Skeeter. Everyone understood each other real well. I wondered how long it would be before Slim appeared at the door of the Winnebago. Earl was cousin Buddy's lover. He noticed the obvious attraction between the two Buddies, but didn't seem to mind. Slim and Earl both appreciated the fully outfitted camper. The motels in town were filled with police and FBI. There was a need for a quiet getaway.

Earl offered to take me to the Temple site, so I left my Mom and Aunts in Lonnie and Skeeter's hands. In the rear view mirror of the Chief's cruiser I could see the two Buddies taking off for the farm.

"We were a minute of two away from being blown up here," Earl said. "Thanks for the warning. I should have thought of that myself. It would fit the M.O."

"Are there any locals who have a real problem with authority?" I asked. "I'm not sure they originally intended to kill policemen and emergency workers, but it seems to me, the guy who did it may have acquired a taste for it."

"You may be right. I've told my men to be careful," Earl replied. "The church building is booby trapped. We've found two more devices."

"No one hurt?"

"No one, but it makes the investigation of the site a bit slow," Earl continued. "We've arrested all the usual suspects. My guys were none too delicate, but I think they are a dry hole. The State Troopers have a list of anti government people, you know, the guys who send threatening letters to the Governor and the like. They are going after them." We got to the site of the church. It was nothing but smoldering rubble, surrounded by a ring of fire engines, police cars and emergency vehicles.

Earl introduced me to some of the firemen and then went off to talk to a ATF agent. A young volunteer fireman came up to me.

"Are you the guy called Clydesdale?" He asked.

"Yep."

"I'm a friend of Jim," he said. "He described you. I guessed it was you." Jim was the kid I played with when I was pruning my Mom's shrubs a month earlier. "I'm Keith. Jim said he had a really good time with you."

"I had a good time with Jim too."

"Jim and I were talking about the bombing. The one in Richmond, not this one," Keith said. He had a slight air of being proud that his own small town had it's own bombing. This would be the first time Victoriaville would ever be on the national news. "Jim couldn't think of anyone mean enough to do something this bad." He paused. "I could."

"Let's have names," I said. "Too many dead people here to play games."

"You're right about that, I came damn near to being one of them when the church blew," Keith said. "Do you remember the Johnson boys? You may have been in school with them."

It took a second, but I remembered them. They were a few years older than me and they had liked bullying the younger smaller kids, about the time I was in fifth grade. "Was that Carlton and Bart Johnson?" I asked.

"Yep," Keith said. "They live in an isolated farm about six miles to the west of here. Mean as snakes. They spent some time at the Victory Temple, but not at the services. Jim's sister found out from a girl she knew. They had the hots for one of the girls there, a fourteen year old. Apparently the Preacher had told them they could have her."

"What does that have to do with the bombing?" I asked.

"Nothing directly, but the Preacher asked the girl to go with them and he said, the guys had done a lot for the Temple. He referred to one of the brothers as, "Nitro man"," Keith said. "The girl thought he said "Night-o man", but Jim figured it was "Nitro". It ain't much, but it might be worth looking into."

"Is that why you are talking to me?"

"It doesn't seem to be enough to tell the police, but it seemed I should tell someone," Keith replied.

"I think your right about that. I'll check on it."

Keith got closer to me and whispered, "Jim said you two had a really good time when you got together." I took a long look at him. He was young, maybe 21, but he sure was fully grown. "Are you staying at your Mom's?" he asked.

"Actually I am bunking in the Winnebago next door in the lot beside her house. I'll be busy until late, but drop in if you're out wandering after 10:00 or so," I said. He went back to the smoldering ruins. I pulled out my cell phone and called the office, asking them to do a search on Carlton and Bart Johnson.

Earl returned. He had never heard of the men. They had no run ins with the law. Earl had been here for about ten years and he wouldn't have known the school bullies. The ATF men were happy with what they found. They were sure some of the same materials used in the Richmond bombs were used here.

Earl took me home. Lonnie and Skeeter were all but members of my family by the time I got back. Skeeter was one of those guys who had been taught to be real polite around ladies. He also was really appreciative of home made food and Mom and Ellen loved to cook. One was always with Edith, but somehow they had made an apple pie and were working on a pot roast for dinner.

Skeeter was big and a stranger in town. Having him prowling around the house was useful, if the murderer was watching, he wouldn't know what Skeeter was. It was the death penalty for killing a cop in Virginia and Skeeter could have been undercover.

I watched Edith while Mom and Ellen ate with Lonnie and Skeeter. I like my Mom's food, but I never approached Skeeter's level of appreciation. I realized he must not have had much of a family life growing up. Sitting with Edith for an hour and a half was good for me. I had always dislike the woman who had always been a sour bitch, but she was so pathetic I felt sorry for her. Being a bitch and stupid wasn't the same thing as being criminal. I wondered if her face would be scarred.

She had been handsome in a horsey way. Even for a woman in her early 70s, being scarred would be horrible for her. She moaned.

"I'm here, Aunt Edith," I said. "It's Clydesdale. Momma and Aunt Ellen are downstairs if you need them."

"I've been a fool," she whimpered. "He was a false prophet. I thought he was a Saint."

"He was behind the bombings in Richmond, Edith," I said. "Do you know who helped him?"

"No one could have possibly done anything that awful," she said.

"Buddy's wife was helping," I said. "You know that, don't you?"

"I can't believe it," she moaned, but a trace of her normal sanctimoniousness in her voice. I decided to take a flier.

"Could Carlton and Bart Johnson been involved?" I asked.

"Oh God," she said, "Oh no! That's why they were there! I saw them once in awhile with the Preacher. They were trash and I thought they had reformed, but they never came to services. Bart was in the Army. He was in a bomb squad. Dishonorable discharge. We never learned why." Edith seemed to have exhausted herself.

I left the room and called Mom to replace me at Edith's side. I raced to the Winnebago and called my office, telling them about the bomb squad info. The computer geeks had discovered the Army records and the discharge, but not the reason. I called Earl and told him.

Earl had not been resting. He had done some work on the Johnson brothers and was not at all happy with what he found. "I'm putting a watch on their farm. It's dark already, I'll go in tomorrow morning for a search," Earl said. "Slim was downright pissed he hadn't thought of them right off. Odd characters."

I went back to the house. Skeeter and Lonnie was going to spend the night there, with Lonnie at the back door and Skeeter at the front. I was to stay in the Winnebago to maintain contact with my office. Ellen and Lonnie were working on brownies. Ellen and Mom switched places and Mom told me of

Edith's ramblings. The Johnson brothers were the focus of her thoughts. I went back to the mobile home.

Keith must have been waiting for me to leave the house. He wandered by on the side walk and said, "Hi,". It was as if we had met by accident. I asked him in. He eagerly accepted. He was dressed in a tee shirt and shorts. I had no real idea what he looked like under the Fireman's equipment. He was football player muscular, dark hair, with a small mustache. His shorts were cut off jeans. His cock and balls were clearly indicated by wear marks.

He was nervous and excited. I could see his cock growing as I closed the door.

"Jim said, you were real nice," Keith said.

"Is he a good friend of yours?"

"Yes," Keith answered.

"How close are you?" I asked lowering my voice.

"I guess about as two guys can get," he said. He began to whisper. "Jim told me all about you and what you did, but he had to go back to school before we had a chance to try them out."

"You want to try something now?" I asked.

"I've been thinking about it every night since Jim left."

Part 18

Keith got better as he stripped. He was beefy and muscular, with a coating of fine hair on his chest and a treasure trail to his pubic bush. There was a treasure poking from the bush, a thick tube of uncut meat. Keith was not what I expected. He was inexperienced, but more than eager. He liked sex and he loved man sex.

It was rare to find a guy so inexperienced, but with no hang ups. He and Jim had sucked some, but that was the extent of his knowledge. But, the sky was the limit when it came to his willingness.

He was a cock hound and size queen. He thought he had found the mother load of cocks the minute he saw my dick. It took me a good two or three seconds to realize I had discovered a first rate sexual athlete, inexperienced, but ready for training. He deep throated me on the first effort.

Eventually, I pried him loose from my cock and sucked his dick. It was hard and dripping. I worked a finger to the rear and touched his hole. He shivered in excitement and opened wide.

"You like being fucked?" I asked.

"Never been fucked, but I'm pretty sure I'll like it," Keith replied. "You're awfully big, but I figure I might as well start at the top. Jim said it was incredible."

"What makes you think you would like it?" I asked as I worked a finger into his ass. There was no resistance, no effort to exclude my finger. I rammed his prostate. Keith moaned in pleasure as another shiver of excitement ran through his body. I had to admit, Keith was ready and willing. I just wasn't sure he was able.

Fifteen minutes later I knew the answer. By that time I had been deep fucking him for ten minutes. There had been one or two little rough spots in the road at the beginning, but they faded the deeper into his ass my cock penetrated. He liked long deep strokes the best, but he didn't mind short quick thrusts, especially if my cock head was in the vicinity of his prostate.

He liked it spread eagle and doggy style. If it involved my cock and his ass hole, Keith was game. It was nice. It was pure enjoyment, all sexual excitement for Keith. He must have shot off four or five times. These were not modest dick dribbles. Keith was 23 and he must have been saving up for years to produce the cock gushers.

There was sperm everywhere after each orgasm. My chest was covered in ribbons of cum. As I said. Keith was a cum hound. I left my loads ten inches into his ass, so he had to meet his needs by licking up his own from my chest and gut. This worked out well.

He would shoot and I would follow. While I was recovering, he would lick me clean. By the time he was done, we were ready to go again. This went on until Skeeter came out to tell me Aunt Edith was talking. He walked in on us fucking. I pulled out of Keith, turned the boy over to him and went inside.

Edith was in pain, the shock had warn off and she was feeling terrible. She also wanted revenge. The pain must have cleared her mind.

"All those dead people, the Johnson's could have done it," she said. "They were miserable little boys and young men. I remember some folks thought their stint in the army would have helped them. It didn't. They came out meaner and nastier."

"They liked women, but it wasn't right," Edith continued. "I think several women of the church went out with them. I didn't understand that at all. The Preacher must have made them do it."

"You think he was pimping for them?" Aunt Ellen asked. Ellen wasn't prone to mince words.

"That could have been," Edith replied, "I have been such a fool! I thought it was odd and didn't say anything about it."

"They might have killed you," Ellen said. "They seemed to kill anyone who could lead the authorities to them."

"I'd rather be dead than thought of as a gullible fool," Edith said.

"Don't be silly, Edith," Ellen replied. "You have been a fool, but can redeem yourself if you help to put them where they belong. Being gullible isn't a crime. Not helping the authorities is."

"What do you know about Rev. Tommy?" I asked. I wanted to know if there were any additional links to the TV Evangelist in Charlotte. We talked for an hour. Edith wasn't a perceptive woman, she was a gossip, busybody.

She had not put things together in a pattern, but she had seen a lot. She interpreted things to favor those she liked and to put those she disliked in the least favorable light possible. I realized she would be a good witness, since she had seen many minor incidents that could be used to corroborate other peoples' testimony.

Mom and Ellen took good notes. I went back to the Winnebago. Skeeter returned to the house, I returned to Keith's ass. I fucked him again, then told him I had to get some sleep. He went home, but promised to come back.

The phone rang at five. It was Earl. The Johnson boys were getting ready to leave. There was a big bang on the phone and it went dead. The Johnson's lived outside of town on the side of a mountain. I looked in that general direction and saw a pink cloud of smoke and flame rising from the area of the Johnson house. The town fire alarm was blowing, waking the volunteer firemen. Seconds later, it seemed as if the entire town was up, lights were on in almost every window.

Much to my surprise, I jumped into Mom's car and drove in the direction of the explosion. I could see secondary explosions on the hill and guessed the Johnson's arsenal was blowing up. I wanted to call Earl and see if he was all right, but guessed he was too busy and I was better to keep the lines open.

I couldn't get close. The Troopers had sealed off the roads up the mountain, so I parked the car and walked in. It was still dark. I could hear the fire engines' sirens, punctuated by small explosions. It took about 20 minutes to get to the area near the Johnson house. I found Earl behind his cruiser.

The woods were on fire and there was no sign of the Johnson house. No one could fight the fire yet because ammunition was exploding from the heat of the fire.

"No one's hurt," Slim said. He was huddled beside Earl. "Except for the Johnsons and whoever was holed up in the house. I was pretty sure I saw four men near the car just before it blew."

The rest of the night was confused. They got the fire under control and found a grand total of four bodies.

A week later the full extent of the plot was known and eventually a slew of born-again, self righteous fools found themselves doing serious jail time. The Mayor of Richmond and the so called, "Christian" Police Chief were out of power. The Mayor would have to face serious Obstruction of Justice charges, but he had a near total physical and mental breakdown.

The next day Skeeter, Lonnie and I cruised out to Cousin Buddy's farm to pick up our Buddy and get home. When we got to the farm, Earl's police cruiser was in the yard as was a pick-up with volunteer fireman's plates.

I walked into the kitchen and found the two Buddies, Earl, Keith and Jim drinking coffee. Jim had come back from college, because of the excitement. Everyone introduced himself and we had a nice, fill in the gaps conversation.

Dental records identified the Johnsons, DNA a guy from Charlotte and much to my surprise, the Preacher. The Johnsons were burned alive as was the accomplice from Charlotte. The Preacher had been killed earlier. He was found dismembered. Portions of his body had been burned up in a wood stove, the trunk and head remained. Apparently the Johnsons were getting rid of the evidence.

The Preacher had died from loss of blood. Coroner said, the dismemberment apparently began before the Preacher died. That fool had been playing with psychotic killers and got caught up in it.

The final explosion was an accident. When it comes to poetic justice, it doesn't get any better than this. The reign of terror was over and the perpetrators died in as painful and horrible way as anyone could have wished. I would never wish being burned alive on anyone, but for this crew it seemed fitting.

I said, we needed to get back to Richmond.

"Do you have a few minutes for some rest and relaxation?" Cousin Buddy asked. "My kids are coming back tonight and this may be my last chance for fun in a while." He tried to sound as if this was a spur of the moment comment, but I realized what Jim and Keith were there for.

"That sure sounds good to me," I said.

"Me too," Earl added. He looked at Keith, who he didn't know. Earl wasn't sure Keith was a member of the fraternity. Keith cupped his basket and gave it a good squeeze. "Let's all get naked and play. Is anything out of bounds?"

"Well, I guess I'm the only one here who has been with everyone here," I said. "Everyone is tried and tested and has passed all the tests with flying colors."

"Hot damn!" Earl said. We went upstairs and stripped. Earl formed a nice fuck group with the two Buddies. They made a ring of shifting penetrations.

Lonnie hit it off with Keith. I played with Jim, while Skeeter spent most of the time on his knees, sucking whichever cock came into range. I was deep into Jim's ass when Skeeter began to lick at my ass. I had Jim bent double and stretched wide open. I spread my legs as wide as I could and Skeeter wedged himself in the gap.

My balls were slapping against Jim's balls and Skeeter got to suck all four of the nuts. Jim shot a spectacular load after a few minutes of this treatment. I was just beginning to get into it and wasn't going to shoot for a while. Pulled out of Jim and motioned to Earl the come over.

I figured Skeeter would like having the Chief of Police's cock in his ass. I guessed right. Earl was a big boy, but less massive than me and I wanted him to loosen Skeeter up a bit before I went in. It was a good plan, but they liked it a bit too much. I was without a partner. I saw Cousin Buddy on the bed. He looked at me, I looked at him. He pulled his legs up on the edge of the bed, spread them, then winked his ass hole at me.

I wandered over to him. "Do you think you can take it?" I asked.

"I think so," Buddy said. "I've been getting some practice."

"Has it been good?"

"A lot better than I thought it could be," Buddy replied. I nosed my cock into his pink hole. My head barely penetrated his sphincter when I pulled it out and added some lubricant. I had known Buddy since being a kid and it seemed strange to be fucking him. I got in position again and popped my head into the hole. The other Buddy was behind me and bumped me. I went in to the hilt.

Buddy had been primed by Earl and the other Buddy and his ass was a hot furnace. His ass clamped shut on my cock, trapping it in his chute. He had a sphincter of iron, but the chute was filled with lube mixed with Earl and Buddy's cock juices. It felt really good. Buddy's ass was contracting and quivering.

I don't know when exactly it happened, but Buddy and I merged. He suddenly relaxed and I slipped deeper and my cock became a part of his ass. It was as if my dick had found a home. My cock became hypersensitive and every movement of his quivering ass gave me overwhelming feelings of pleasure. Every move I made left him gasping for breath. It was total sexual union. His ass just quivered until I shot off my load deeper in any man's ass than ever before. The other Buddy was there to suck my Cousin as he came. I pulled out, then we lay in bed. I rear ended him and we stayed in bed, twitching and enjoying.

Keith and Buddy were spread eagle on the floor while Earl and Jim slow fucked them. For the first time since the bombing in Richmond, I could relax. It seemed as if the cares of the world were dissipated as we fucked and sucked.

About the Author

Bob Archman has lived in Virginia for years, and uses his knowledge of the area to provide the setting for this story. Middle aged, he is bearded, bald and hairy. Bob is interested in ordinary, gay men who do their jobs well, and lead their lives in rural areas and small cities, miles away from the Media's vision of hyper gay life in New York and San Francisco. He is interested in men who are cops, construction workers, firemen, farmers and professionals who happen to be gay. As his detective Clydesdale Noland once remarked when looking at a leather clad biker, "Damn, that's a lot of stuff to take off before you get down to business!"

www.ingramcontent.com/pod-product-compliance
Lightning Source LLC
Chambersburg PA
CBHW051123260626
47170CB00005B/1640